CROSSING BORDERS

CROSSING BORDERS

MICHAEL HARTWIG

Herring Cove Press

ISBN: 978-0-578-96345-7

Second Edition 2024

This is a work of fiction. Names, characters, businesses, places, events, locales, and incidents are either the products of the author's imagination or used in a fictitious way.

Any resemblance to actual persons, living or dead, or actual events, is purely coincidental.

Cover Art - Photo by Author

Contents

I

Chapter One

Bernard skied off the top of the lift and slid to a gentle stop overlooking the landscape before him. A beautiful trail with modest pitch followed the contours of the mountain below. He stood in the bright sunlight, breathed in the crisp air, and took in the breathtaking view of the Eiger looming in the near distance, a sheer-faced peak that overlooked snow fields, forests, and the extensive resort of Grindelwald.

The trail directly in front of him had been heavily skied in the morning, leaving large moguls and slick icy spots along much of the run. An alternative route, to the left, was steeper but still had fresh powder. Bernard adjusted his goggles, put the straps of his ski poles around his wrists, and pushed off. He carved a few quick turns and then turned left, feeling the adrenaline rush through his body as he leaped over the ridge and made carefully edged turns on the steeper slope.

Soon he was making smooth parallel turns, a rhythmic dance across the snow, turning one direction then swiveling to the other.

The trail curved and divided, one fork leading to the bottom of the lift and the other through a forest to another set of lifts and trails. Bernard headed toward the forest, making a few quick carved turns before entering the narrower path.

In the distance, he noticed a pink jacket in a thicket of trees at the side of the trail. As he approached, he realized a young girl had fallen into a ravine. He skidded to a stop at the edge of the trail and yelled to her in German, "*Bist du verletzt* – are you hurt?"

The little girl, about eight, was crying. She nodded yes.

"*Kannst du aufstehen* – can you get up?" he inquired.

She tried to stand, but fell quickly back into the deep snow and nodded no.

Bernard's heart raced as he realized how serious the girl's situation was. Bernard kicked off his skis and walked toward her. "*Wie heißt du?*" he asked as he reached her.

She replied her name was Zoe, Zoe Decker. Bernard asked where her parents were, and she began to cry. "*Ich bin verloren* – I am lost."

Bernard asked if he could touch her leg, and Zoe nodded yes. "*Tut es weh?*" he asked whether it hurt. Zoe nodded yes again.

Bernard pulled out his cell phone and dialed the emergency number for the ski patrol. An operator answered, and he explained that he had found a girl hurt on the run to Tschuggen and that she needed help right away. He gave the operator her name in case her parents were looking for her, and he said he would wait for the patrol with her.

Bernard slipped his phone into his vest pocket and then asked Zoe, "*Darf ich dein Bein berühren?*"

Zoe nodded that he could touch her leg. Some of Bernard's friends had convinced him several years earlier to take a course in Reiki, a form of energy healing. He was skeptical at first, but during the seminar, he found he was more intuitive than he had imagined and seemed to have had a gift for healing. He traced some Reiki symbols on his hands and held her leg at the place where it looked injured.

He could feel a warm tingling pass through his hands, and heat begin to radiate around the wound. The gentle touch made Zoe relax, and Bernard wondered if the pain was subsiding. A few moments later, two ski patrols showed up with a sled and walked through the heavy snow toward them. They asked some questions and then lifted her up and laid her on the sled, wrapping her snugly with blankets.

One patrol turned to Bernard and said in English, "Thanks for stopping to help her. Her parents have contacted the dispatch office, and they are going to meet us at the clinic in town. We can take care of things from here."

In German, Bernard replied, "If you don't mind, I would like to stay with her and make sure she's okay."

"That's fine," one of them replied. "By the way, your German is excellent. What's your name?"

"Bernard, Bernard Williams."

"You can follow us. We'll ski down to the Grund train station, where an ambulance is waiting."

Bernard stepped into his skis and followed the patrol, who carefully skied down the trail with Zoe in tow. At the station, the patrol laid Zoe in the back of an emergency vehicle, and Bernard took a seat next to her and laid his skis down on the floor. She looked up at him in fright. He placed his hand on her arm and said, "You're going to be fine. We will see your parents in just a few minutes." She smiled.

As they pulled up to the small clinic, Bernard noticed through the ambulance window two frantic parents standing on the curb next to a nurse holding their hands. All three peered into the windows of the vehicle to get a glimpse of Zoe. The driver parked and opened the back hatch. The two parents ran to the car and yelled, "Zoe, Zoe – are you okay? We're so sorry we lost you. Oh, darling."

Zoe's mother wiped tears from her eyes, and her father held the woman's hand, an anxious look on his face as the nurse helped the driver unload the stretcher. They wheeled Zoe into the reception of the clinic, where a physician approached Zoe and examined her.

He touched her gently, feeling the contours of her legs. Sliding the bottom of her ski pants up, the doctor shook his head and said, "I'm afraid this looks like a fracture. I'd like to get some x-rays, and then we will know better what needs to be done."

The parents nodded as the physician and nurse wheeled Zoe through some doors deeper into the clinic. They then turned to Bernard and said, in English, "Thank you so much for finding our daughter and making sure she got care. We're so grateful."

In German Bernard responded, "I'm glad I showed up shortly after she fell. There were hardly any others on the trail so late in the afternoon."

The man, now looking intently at Bernard, said, "Oh, you speak German. I thought you were American."

"I am," Bernard said, extending his hand. "I am Bernard Williams."

"Theo, Theo Decker," the man said in reply, shaking Bernard's hand forcefully. "And this is my wife, Jules."

Bernard nodded to them, feeling slightly intimidated by the tall, imposing Swiss man. His black and red ski jacket, dark pants, and gray ski boots made him look even more formidable. He had intense, deeply set hazel eyes, an angular face, and dark blonde tousled hair. His round nose, full lips, and dimples softened his other features, giving him a teddy-bear look.

Jules looked more French than Swiss. She had caramel skin, shiny brunette hair, and dark brown eyes, made more alluring by her arched brows and long lashes. She wore a stylish light blue and turquoise jacket and dark blue pants.

"Are you here on a ski holiday from the States?" Theo asked.

"Yes, I've just been here a couple of days."

"Your German is impeccable. Do you come here often?"

"No, this is only my second time in Grindelwald."

"Where did you learn German so well?" Jules asked.

"In school and with my work."

Theo gave an inquisitive look, encouraging Bernard to continue.

"I was a recruiter of foreign students for a university in Boston," Bernard elaborated.

"And what do you do now?" Jules pressed further.

Bernard hesitated. It was a painful question, having just been laid off after 20 years of service. "I'm in between jobs at the moment," he said stoically.

"Oh," Jules replied apologetically for having touched upon what seemed like a sensitive point.

Theo wrung his hands nervously as they waited for the physician to return with Zoe. Jules hung onto his arm, trying to calm him. Bernard noticed their distress and tried to continue the conservation, "So, are you from here?"

Theo seemed relieved to be given the chance to talk more. "We're from Bern. Or, I should say, I am from Bern, and my wife is from Geneva, though her parents are from France."

"And do you come to Grindelwald often?"

"Yes, we have a home here."

"That must be nice!" Bernard noted with a smile.

"Yes, we're very fortunate to be able to enjoy the mountains."

"And what do you do?" Bernard inquired, looking at them both.

"Jules works with a pharmaceutical company, and I'm in the government," Theo said.

Bernard's brows arched upward, and he asked, "What do you do there?"

"I'm in special international relations. We foster collaborative relationships with other governments around politics, economy, cultural exchanges, and things like that."

"That's fascinating!"

"It sounds more interesting than it is," Theo said playfully.

At that point, the physician came out into the lobby with Zoe in a wheelchair. Theo and Jules turned attentively to him, waiting for his diagnosis.

"Well, Mr. and Mrs. Decker, your daughter is fortunate. The x-rays show no evidence of a fracture. In fact, I'm a little dumbfounded. Even the bruising seems to have subsided since her arrival here. There are some scrapes where she hit a tree, and the initial report of the patrol suggests that she should have had a fracture. But I've taken several images, and I see nothing. It's great news. She should ice the area and then heat it. Do you have a heating pad and ice packs at home?"

Theo nodded yes.

"Apply ice, then heat, and repeat. Keep her off her feet for the first 24 hours and then let me know if there are any complications. Otherwise, I think all she needs is a new jacket and a new pair of ski pants!" He smiled at Zoe.

Zoe smiled back, and then nodded warmly toward Bernard, acknowledging his role in her good outcome.

"Well, young lady," Bernard began in German, holding Zoe's hands, "it was a pleasure to meet you, although I wish the circumstances had been different. I hope to see you on the slopes again – but on the trail, not off!"

She laughed, and Theo and Jules smiled. Theo looked over at Jules with an inquisitive look. She nodded and Theo asked, "Bernard, if you are free this evening, we'd love to invite you to our place for dinner – to thank you."

Bernard hesitated, and Jules jumped in, "Sorry, we'd also like to invite your wife as well."

"Thank you, but I'm recently divorced. I'm here on my own."

"Well then, you must come. We insist!" she added enthusiastically.

Bernard paused and then said, "Okay. Sure. What can I bring?"

"Nothing. You're our guest! What's your phone number? I'll text our address," Theo said.

Bernard gave him his number and, a few moments later, a text from Theo popped up with their address. "Is 6:30 good?" Theo asked further.

"Perfect, see you then."

Bernard shook their hands, pressed his hand on top of Zoe's, and winked at her. He left the clinic, grabbed his skis outside, and walked to his apartment.

The sky had become overcast and darker, and a light snow began to fall, specks of white and gold caught playfully in the glow of streetlights. Wooden chalets and hotels lined the main street where, on the first floor, brightly lit ski shops displayed colorful jackets, equipment, and accessories. The sidewalks were full of skiers heading home or meeting friends at local bars. From time to time, breaks in the clouds made it possible to see the peaks that towered over the town center – a curtain of glacier studded crests that were the draw for so many tourists.

Bernard took a small path up the hill, clinging to a handrail to prevent slipping on the compacted snow and ice. As he got farther from the town center, it became quieter, and he could hear the snowflakes landing on his jacket. He arrived at a traditional Swiss chalet – a four-story wooden structure with carved balconies and a beamed roof - where he had rented an apartment on the top floor. He climbed the interior stairs and slipped the key into the door of his unit. Once inside, he slipped off his ski boots, hung his skis on the rack, and walked into the living room, turning on a few table lamps.

The apartment was spacious, with large glass windows overlooking the Eiger Mountain. The unit was furnished in upscale Swiss décor - carved wooden chairs, a comfortable sofa, and thick area rugs. On one wall, there was a sizeable stone fireplace with an alcove full of freshly cut wood. To the left of the living area, there was a generous dining table set in front of a window looking out over a grove of fir trees laden with snow. The unit had a modern kitchen and a utility area replete with a washing machine and space to hang clothes.

Bernard walked down the hall and went into the marble bathroom. He looked into the mirror and used his fingers to put a few errant locks of dark hair back in place. His face had already begun to tan in the mountain sun, and he rubbed some cream around his dark brown eyes to reduce the growing creases. He slipped off his sweater and the underlying thermal layer and turned sideways to check his physique. He was in good shape for 50. He had a well-defined hairy chest and taut abdomen. He was lean and muscular but preoccupied with the advancing signs of middle age – a few strands of gray hair around his temples and the loss of muscle mass here and there.

He walked into the large bedroom that faced another range of peaks and rummaged through the armoire for a fresh pair of jeans, shirt, and sweater. He changed clothes and went back into the living room, poured himself a glass of wine, and sat down to check emails.

His daughter, Angela, had sent questions about train connections. She was planning a visit in a week during one of her college breaks. His ex-wife, Susan, had sent some more documents for him to sign, bringing to a close the arrangements for their divorce.

It had been a difficult summer and fall. The university where Bernard had been an effective recruiter for foreign students from the Middle East and Europe wanted to shift direction and recruit more from Asia. They brought in new younger staff with language and cultural expertise more suitable for finding students in China, India, Japan, and Indonesia. Just after losing his job, his wife announced she wanted a divorce, moving in shortly thereafter with a professor from another college.

Bernard hadn't anticipated how reassuring a mountain vacation would be for him. The looming peaks rising from the valley floor reverberated a sense of solidity and strength, a feeling of impregnability and permanence during a time when everything had been kicked out from under him and was in flux.

He always worried that Susan would meet someone overseas during business trips for the aerospace company she worked for. He never noticed the friendliness between her and Charles. In fact, she seemed bored when he, a political scientist, began tortuous analyses of political issues. Charles was thin, frail, and bookish. Susan was typically attracted to more athletic types. Bernard had been surprised when she first flirted with him, Bernard, at a gathering of colleagues in Cambridge twenty something years ago. He still remembered the unusual warmth of a mid-September evening, people spilling out onto a stone patio, sharing stories of summer travels. He had combined a recruiting trip with a week's vacation along the Turkish coast and was busy describing new Roman excavations at Ephesus with an archaeologist from Harvard. Alan had an exotic allure - tousled sun-bleached hair, a perpetual two-day growth of a beard framing a handsome face, and an imposing body that filled a room with warmth and energy. Bernard noticed Susan from across the patio, convinced she was interested in Alan. He was used to being the invisible one, overlooked by beautiful women drawn to more handsome and professionally intriguing men. For once, he found that the woman everyone was staring at was interested in him and, much to his chagrin, the man was, too. It was almost comical how they vied for his attention. By the end of the evening, he had numbers for both and called Susan the next week.

They began to date. He expected her to lose interest, to find him too vanilla, to want more than he could give. He was sexually awkward, never at ease in his own body, much less with someone else's. Unimaginative sexually, Bernard let Susan lead, her arousal contagious. Gradually, he felt more confident and self-assured.

Now he wondered what would have happened had he called Alan. At the time, he hardly gave it a consideration. He was neither daring nor unconventional. Alan was handsome, and the idea of a man's body wasn't entirely disgusting, but whenever he considered the notion, he felt an unsettled stirring in the pit of his stomach. Later, Alan came back from Turkey with a boyfriend – intense and combustible. They fought, and Ahmed was sent back to Istanbul. At the time, Bernard was grateful for stability and convention, now he longed for something a little more adventuresome.

Susan was an avid skier, perhaps even more accomplished than Bernard. It was their common interest that helped solidify their relationship and kept it fresh. Early in their romance, they escaped to Vermont and New Hampshire to ski, meeting friends on the slopes and snuggling in front of a crackling fire at the end of the day. When their daughter Angela was three, they gave her ski lessons. She loved winter adventures with her parents and took well to the sport. She was so cute in her little ski jacket, gloves, helmet, and skis. She was intrepid, racing down expert slopes with aplomb.

As years progressed, weekends in the mountains became larger gatherings of families – all with kids. Out went the romantic evenings by the fire. Instead, exhausted, they fell into bed only to rise to a house full of guests, pancakes to make, and gear to organize before the shuttle to the slopes. Bernard embraced the idea that lovers could become friends, companions, and partners and that their sex lives would become less important, intermittent. As Angela and her friends matured, Bernard and Susan could again enjoy quieter dinner parties with friends and more focused time with each other. Until the end, their lovemaking had been regular, even if not particularly creative or passionate. Now overlooking this idyllic alpine setting, Bernard still couldn't make sense of her abrupt departure – the indifference and antipathy that invaded what had seemed to be a happy and satisfying marriage.

When he announced that he was going to Switzerland for two months, friends were worried about his emotional health and made plans to join him later. Sure, he felt sad, even melancholy, but he looked forward to a new start, a chance to live abroad, cross over to another world, step into a new identity – whatever that might be. He had nothing holding him back, no ties except his daughter, a blank canvas waiting to be painted.

Bernard grabbed a bottle of wine from the side table and put on his jacket, hat, and gloves, and headed out the door and down a winding path toward Theo's and Jules' apartment near the town church. He rang their bell, and Zoe opened the door, grinning with excitement.

"Good evening, Zoe. How are you feeling?"

"Better, thank you. We applied ice and heat to the leg, and it feels much better."

"I'm glad to hear."

Theo walked up behind her and offered to take Bernard's coat. Bernard handed him the wine and shook his hand.

"Welcome. We're glad you could make it."

Jules entered from the kitchen and walked over to Bernard, giving him a traditional warm welcome of kisses on both cheeks. "*Bienvenue*, Bernard!" A subtle fragrance lingered. She wore tight jeans and a soft low-cut merino wool sweater revealing full round breasts.

"*Merci pour l'invitation*," he said in reply.

"*Ah, vous parlez français?*"

"*Oui, bien sûr. Tu peux me tutoyer*," he said, inviting her to use the familiar form with her.

"No need to thank us for the invitation. We're so grateful for what you did for Zoe this afternoon. Please, come into the living room," Theo said, pointing toward a large living area.

A crackling fire cast an orange glow on a sofa and two comfortable chairs encircling a low coffee table in front of the stone mantle. Theo invited Bernard to take a seat, and Jules brought in a platter of cheese and *crostini*.

"Some wine?" Theo asked Bernard.

"Yes, please. Perhaps red?"

Theo reached for an open bottle on a narrow oak sideboard and poured him a generous glass. He was wearing a dark pair of jeans and a black stretch pullover with the arms pulled slightly up his forearm. As he handed Bernard the glass of wine, the contours of his muscular arms and shoulders became more pronounced, pressing against the stretchy fabric.

"*Salute!*" they all said in unison.

"So, are you here by yourself or with some friends?" Theo began.

"By myself. I needed a break after the divorce and the sudden employment change."

"What a great place to escape," Jules said with a heavy French accent. "How long are you here?"

"For a couple of months," Bernard said as he reached toward the cheese platter to take a small slice of Gruyere.

"Wow!" Theo said excitedly. "Now that's a ski trip!"

Bernard nodded, taking a sip of the wine.

"So, you recruit foreign students?" Jules continued. "That must be why you are so good at languages."

"Well, it has been a good way to use my language skills."

"So, are you looking at other schools for a new position?" Theo asked.

"Yes, and I'm considering similar work in other venues."

"We might have to recruit you," Theo said, winking at Bernard.

"Hmm," Bernard murmured. "I'm not sure how that would work. I'm too old to start a new profession."

"What do you mean, too old? You look like you're in your forties – a good age for our kind of work."

"I'm 50!"

Theo's brows arched up. "I would have never guessed. Well, we're always looking for mature candidates."

The word 'mature' stung as Bernard processed its implications.

"Thanks, but no thanks," Bernard said and then added, "Politics was never my thing."

Theo didn't reply, but he seemed to ponder the idea, staring into the fire. Jules then said, "And do you have children?"

"One daughter, Angela. She's at Brown University. She's coming for a visit next week."

"We'd love to meet her. Maybe we can introduce her to some of our neighbors' children who are also college age," Jules said excitedly.

"That would be nice, but I don't want to bother you."

"It's not a bother," Jules said warmly.

As Jules and Bernard discussed Angela and her plans, Theo observed Bernard carefully. He had inherited his English parents' dark hair, high cheekbones, perfectly proportioned nose, and a lean frame. His maternal grandmother was Italian, so he had a darker complexion than most New Englanders. A dark stubble circled his mouth and lined his chin and jaw. As the conversation continued, Bernard was more and more aware of Theo's gaze and looked over from time to time, catching his eyes.

They moved into the dining area where Bernard sat across from Zoe, who continued to grin at him and rock her legs under the table with joy. Theo sat to Bernard's left, and Jules shuttled between the kitchen and the table, bringing in a large platter with a pastry-encrusted pork tenderloin surrounded by roasted vegetables.

"This looks and smells amazing," Bernard said.

"It's one of my favorites. I coated the pastry on the inside with three types of mustard and a variety of freshly chopped herbs and then sealed it around the meat," Jules explained. She sliced a portion for everyone, and people cut into the tender meat.

"Hmm," Bernard expressed warmly as he took a bite. "Delicious."

"Yes, dear. You did good," Theo said to Jules, raising his glass in a toast.

"So, Jules, you work in pharmaceutics. Do you do much work in Boston?"

"The company I work for is headquartered there – in Cambridge. We have done a lot of work in designing protocols for testing people during epidemics. It's been a lucrative business, given what has transpired the last couple of years."

"What a coincidence, my wife's company had a chance to move in the direction of health care technology, too, but declined and remained in aerospace. It's too bad for them. Arms purchases have declined in favor of environmental infrastructure and health care. They are still doing well as the government supports them, but I imagine they could have done a lot better had they pivoted," Bernard explained.

"Yes, we are surprised the Americans haven't done more to invest in green infrastructure and technology. Everyone else is, and their economies are booming," Theo noted, looking intensely at Bernard.

Theo became noticeably more animated, enthusiastically engaging Bernard in a variety of topics around international culture and politics. Jules became annoyed and decided to wrestle control of the conversation away from Theo. "So, Bernard, why Grindelwald?"

He turned toward her and said, "I came here with some colleagues a couple of years ago, and I couldn't believe it. It is the quintessential Swiss experience – skiing between several car-free villages, stopping at terraced restaurants overlooking some of the most beautiful peaks in the Alps, and enjoying an extensive network of lifts and runs that never gets boring. When I asked myself where I would want to spend two months, this was the place!"

"We don't get too many Americans here in the winter," Theo noted, drawing Bernard's attention back to him.

"Most Americans gravitate to Colorado or Utah, maybe even British Columbia, for skiing. The Alps are appealing, but most think it's too difficult to get here and too expensive once one has arrived. But I've found it's just as easy getting from Boston to Switzerland than going to Utah, and the prices are actually cheaper here."

"I told you!" Theo exclaimed, looking over at Jules. Then he turned toward Bernard and said, "I'm definitely going to recruit you for our international relations efforts. You're a great spokesperson already!"

Bernard blushed.

They eventually finished dinner. Theo and Bernard took plates into the kitchen while Jules helped Zoe get ready for bed. Bernard remarked to himself how oddly familiar and intimate it was standing near Theo, rinsing dishes, loading the dishwasher, and drying pots and pans – as if they had been friends for years. He observed him – an intensely masculine person with a thick muscular frame – yet also warm, friendly, and at ease doing domestic chores.

When Jules returned, she looked preoccupied, glancing at her computer.

Theo took note and said, "Bernard, would you like an after-dinner drink? I think Jules has some emails she has to attend to, but we don't want you to rush off."

"Are you sure?" Bernard inquired. "I don't want to keep you from your evening."

"We're sure," Theo said without equivocation. He led him into the living area and offered him a brandy.

Theo sat on the sofa and Bernard on an adjoining chair, both glaring into the orange embers of the fire. They clinked glasses, and both took an unhurried sip of the brandy.

Theo got up, reached for the fireplace iron, threw several new logs onto the fire, and then stirred the glowing embers. He squatted in front of the mantle, and Bernard couldn't help but notice his firm, round buttocks pressed against the stretchy fabric of his jeans. He got back up and settled into the sofa, stroking the dark blonde hair on his upper arm and swirling the amber liquid in his glass.

"I'm sorry to hear of your divorce," Theo began.

"Yes, it was unexpected. We had been together for 20 years."

"Were there any warnings?"

"None. Everything seemed fine, stable, happy."

"That must have been awful to lose your job and your marriage all in a matter of a few months."

"Indeed. That's why I'm here. I need time to regroup, think, and imagine the future."

Theo smiled and nodded, as if he understood Bernard's dilemma.

An awkward silence ensued until Jules walked in. "Hey men, I just finished my work. Can I join you?"

Both nodded. Jules poured herself a glass of brandy and then settled close to Theo on the sofa. She leaned into his body and put her arm around his shoulder, stroking the back of his head. She took a sip of the brandy and tilted her head toward Bernard with her body still pressed firmly against Theo's. Bernard thought it was a very territorial gesture, almost as if she were warning him against making a move on her husband.

The gesture made him wonder if he had been giving mixed signals over dinner. He found Theo very appealing. He had a commanding presence and a gentle spirit – a killer combination of fierce virility and warm thoughtfulness. He was affable, spoke with a sexy British accent, wore stylish clothes, had an intense gaze, and could carry on interesting conversations about a broad range of topics.

Actually, he had been worried that Theo would find his furtive glances at Jules problematic. He was charmed by her French accent, her pursed lips, luminous skin, and the beautiful brunette hair that laid gently on her sexy shoulder.

In reality, he found them both intriguing, and that unnerved him. Since his divorce, his interest in sex had waned, perhaps a self-protective survival strategy. But as the evening progressed, he felt a wave of sensations rush over him – the solidity and power of Theo's body and the pleasing scent and grace of Jules's. He felt as if he were a vintner who had opened two different bottles of wine and was trying to identify complex textures, colors, and flavors. Both were pleasing, corpulent, and worthy of savoring.

They finished their drinks, and Bernard excused himself, sarcastically trying to convince his hosts that he had a busy day ahead of him.

"Before you leave," Jules began, "I wanted to ask you something."

Bernard nodded.

"Zoe told me you had held her legs earlier on the slopes, and the pain went away."

"Ahh," Bernard nodded. "I did."

"And the doctor was surprised there wasn't a fracture and that the bruising had already subsided."

Theo looked at Bernard with intrigue as Jules continued her questions. Bernard stared back as if to affirm his suspicions and said, "I have some training in Reiki, a form of energy healing. Some say it works, others that it doesn't. I just try to be compassionate and extend as much love and warmth as I can."

"Well, it obviously seemed to have made a big difference," Jules noted. "We're grateful!"

"It's what any parent would do in the same situation."

Theo looked warmly at Bernard and smiled. Jules reached her arm inside Theo's and held him tightly.

"Well, I really must go," Bernard said.

"Let me get your coat," Theo interjected, reaching for it from the hook in the hallway.

He approached Bernard from behind and helped him put his arms into the sleeves, rubbing his shoulders as he adjusted the coat. Bernard thought the gesture was rather intimate for two men, even more so for two men who had just met, but turned and embraced him, nonetheless. Jules gave him kisses on his cheeks.

"I hope we will run into you again on the slopes – although this time *sans urgence*," she said.

"*Oui – sans urgence!*"

"*Auf widersehen*," he said to Theo and "*À bientôt*," to Jules.

"*Alles gut!*" they both said to Bernard as he walked out the door and made his way home.

2

Chapter Two

A few days later, Bernard sat at his dining table with a steaming cup of coffee and a bowl of muesli. He reviewed emails and online papers, all the while glancing out the window at the ever-changing landscape. Fresh snow on the boughs of a pine tree just outside the window glistened in the early rays of light that had broken over the highest peaks. Light puffs of wind blew snow off the branches, creating a glittery white cloud floating to the ground.

Old men came out of their homes to shovel snow and fastidiously rearrange kindling and wood stacked for winter fires. Younger couples marched uphill on snowshoes, leaving fresh prints in the soft whiteness. A cardinal landed on a barren branch of a birch tree, eyeing a ball of seed someone had tied to a wooden fence post below.

Angela sent questions about packing and hinted that mom was doing fine. Life with Charles was good. It still surprised Bernard that his daughter had moved in with Susan rather than stay in her childhood home. It felt like a betrayal, their father-daughter bonding ruptured by an interloper. Charles had other children, but they were married and already away from home. Perhaps Angela thought her mother's and Charles's new relationship would be a distraction, and she would have more freedom.

Bernard responded to some emails from the Boston property manager who checked on the house, cleared snow, and made needed repairs. He thought about selling the family estate but realized there was already too much change to process so, instead, he changed wall colors, remodeled the main bath, and bought new furniture. Jeremy sent pictures of the progress along with invoices that were alarming.

Memories of the dinner with Theo and Jules hovered in the back of his mind, much like an elusive but poignant dream one tries to piece together – Jules – seductive, sensual, territorial - and Theo – strong, imposing, but oddly tender and thoughtful. They played off each other nicely.

These were the first people he had met apart from his and Susan's circle of acquaintances. After the divorce, their friends felt awkward. Invitations diminished, and Bernard felt cut off. Charles was a celebrity scholar, and Susan stepped right into the role of affable and endearing spouse. Many spoke as if she were a trophy wife, a label she didn't seem to mind. He could imagine becoming friends with Theo and Jules – friends he chose, developed, nurtured – not those inherited from his wife. They would be loyal, see his side, show compassion, offer solace. They shared a love of skiing, languages, food, and politics. But, alas, the evening ended with pleasantries and a half-hearted expressed hope to 'run into you one day on the slopes.'

He wondered when they might be back in town and where he was most likely to bump into them. The colors of their ski jackets were etched in his mind – Zoe's light pink coat torn in the fall, Jules's blue jacket with turquoise highlights, and Theo's darker black and red parka.

Bernard finished breakfast and dressed for a day on the slopes, pulling on a soft pair of cotton thermals, long wool ski socks, and his new stretch ski pants and jacket. He spread a light layer of sunscreen on his face.

He checked for all the other accessories – gloves, helmet, goggles, and ski pass. He grabbed skis from the closet and headed out the door. He got to the station a few minutes before the train was scheduled to depart. People lined up, scrutinizing webcams, looking at status lights on the resort display, and doing stretches in place. The early crowd was younger and more serious about skiing, hoping to take advantage of untracked fields of fresh powder. Bernard always skied on the marked trails, but it was fascinating to hear about secret snow fields the locals kept hush for days like this.

The train pulled into the station, and everyone crowded at the doors, ready to jump in. Bernard edged his way forward, placed his skis on the indoor rack, and grabbed a seat. The conductor blew a whistle, and the train pulled out of the station, latching onto the cog track to begin its steep ascent. The route weaved between holiday chalets and summer barns boarded up for the winter. As it rose higher on the slopes, it passed through deep drifts of snow and under special wooden and steel shafts constructed to protect against avalanches.

Higher up, forests of gnarly pines were a testament to the fortitude of nature, adapting to the changing seasons and the vicissitudes of winter storms. The train slowed as it approached Kleine Scheidegg, a small cluster of hotels and restaurants and a connecting station for trains that continued higher up the mountain, bringing tourists to the Jungfrau observatory overlooking Aletsch glacier, Europe's largest.

Bernard disembarked with the other skiers and made his way to a nearby lift that would take them to the top of the Lauberhorn peak, where a variety of runs and off-piste snow fields stretched as far as the eye could see. The early crowd was eager to make tracks in the fresh powder. Bernard mounted a chair with five young men, all actively adjusting boots, poles, gloves, and gear. They kept pointing excitedly at an off-piste area below the lift. He kept looking over at them to see if he could get their attention, strike up a little conversation, but soon realized he was an old man in their eyes – one they deliberately ignored. 'Just wait,' he thought to himself.

At the top of the lift, Bernard looked out over the valley and noticed low-hanging clouds several miles away. He wondered how long the blue skies would last and pushed off eagerly down the slope. He took the trail leading down the famous Lauberhorn race, the longest in Europe. It was a formidable run with a perilous jump, a curvy slope that passed under a train track, and a steep section where it was easy to lose control and venture off the trail. Bernard enjoyed the ideal conditions and stopped periodically to enjoy sensational views of the town of Mürren across the valley, perched on the edge of a cliff overlooking the glacier formed gorge below.

He made his way back to the Lauberhorn lift and, as he approached the summit, clouds began to form. As soon as he started his descent, a frozen fog descended on the slopes. He was already partway down the run when visibility approached zero. Fluorescent markers on the side of the trails, placed precisely for situations like this, showed whether one was on the right or left side of the trail. He clung to the right, listening to crazy local skiers who zipped past, apparently familiar with every dip and curve of the trail. The run was curvy and irregular in pitch, throwing him off from time to time. He began slipping with each turn; the surface becoming increasingly icy.

He began to imagine catastrophic scenarios in his mind, falling off a cliff or running into a tree or a deep snowbank. He remembered a terrible fall a few years back in Stowe in precisely the same conditions. He hadn't expected a sudden shift in terrain and was thrown hard on a patch of ice. He fractured a collarbone and had spent the rest of the season in the lodge. He hoped his Swiss vacation wouldn't end as suddenly. He spotted the dark silhouette of a skier a few meters below him and carefully followed him to the bottom of the run.

"*Scheisse!*" the man yelled as he pulled off his goggles and wiped the nervous perspiration off his forehead.

Bernard affirmed his sentiments in German, "You're absolutely right – shit!"

The adjacent lift slowed to a stop, and both looked at each other in disbelief, wondering how they would get back up to the main area of the mountain. Several meters away, an older lift was still running, and they quickly made their way to the loading area. They nodded sympathetically toward each other, lined up, and grabbed one of the chairs together.

Once on board, they began to chat. Bernard's lift companion, who introduced himself as Hans, realized Bernard wasn't Swiss and began speaking in high German. Eventually they settled into English, which he spoke perfectly, having studied in the UK.

Hans was roughly Bernard's age, but not in as good shape. He clearly enjoyed his daily beer, or two or three. He seemed affable but easily provoked, as witnessed by the cussing episode at the bottom of the trail. He leaned on the safety bar, tired from the tortured run down the icy slope.

Shaking his head, he observed, "The conditions were so good this morning. I came early from Bern."

"They can change quickly."

"You sound familiar with the mountain. Are you a regular?"

"Not really. I was here a few years ago, and I have been here since last Thursday."

"Then you've had great conditions so far. The winters have begun to return to normal. We are all relieved. So, you're from America. What part?"

"Boston."

"Beautiful city – lots of history and charming neighborhoods."

"Do you know it well?"

"Not really. I attended a conference there a few years ago." Hans paused and then continued, "Your German is good. Where did you learn it?"

"In school, although I did an immersion program in Munich."

"I don't detect the usual American twang. Where did you lose it?"

"Here and there," he replied without elaboration.

"So, you like Grindelwald?"

"Yes, it's magnificent – or at least – it usually is!"

They laughed. The lift eventually reached the top where the Eigernordwand lift and the V-Bahn meet. The visibility was still bad, although patches of blue sky appeared from time to time.

"Can I offer you a drink, or maybe we can get some lunch?" Hans asked warmly.

"That would be nice. No need to push off into this."

They walked a few yards toward a stone building that, in clear weather, had incredible views. Inside, the bar was crowded, so they took a seat at a small table near a window. A weathered and stout Swiss woman came up and took their order.

The space was noisy and humid, sweaty skiers removing jackets, helmets, and boots, ready to drink until the poor weather passed. Bernard took his jacket off and draped it on the back of his chair. He leaned over and loosened his boots. He looked up, and Hans was doing the same.

Soon, two beers were placed unceremoniously on the table, followed a few minutes later by two steaming bowls of a local stew. Both dug in.

"You said you had attended a conference in Boston – what kind?" Bernard inquired.

"Oh, something at the Kennedy School of Government – at Harvard."

"Are you in government? Oh, of course, that's a silly question. You live in Bern."

"No, there are other jobs in Bern besides government but, you're right, I work in government."

"What do you do?"

"I'm in strategic international relations."

Bernard gulped. This was Theo's department. What a coincidence, he thought. He hesitated but then asked, "You don't happen to know Theo Decker, do you?"

"Yes, why do you ask?"

"We met last weekend."

"Ah, yes, you must be the American he talked about."

"He mentioned me?"

"Yes, he told the story about Zoe's accident and you coming to her aid. Apparently, you had a nice dinner with him and Jules. You made a good impression. Lucky you, invitations are rare to the Decker household."

Bernard leaned back, took a long sip of beer, and contemplated the new information. "Small world, isn't it?"

"Yes, you have to behave at all times!"

"So, are you and Theo colleagues?"

"More or less. He's higher ranking than I."

"What does that mean?"

"Not much, except that he has more classified access. It doesn't mean much in terms of our work."

"So, have you always worked in the government?"

"No. At one time I was in banking, but when the rules about disclosure of foreign accounts took place, a lot of Swiss banking declined. It was time to look for something else. This job is great as there is so much interest in leveraging international relationships to address our global issues – all very interrelated."

Hans appeared animated and excited about his work – enough to slow his aggressive consumption of the stew. He then paused, looked at Bernard, and asked, "What did you think of Theo and Jules? I've only met Jules a few times, but rumor is that she keeps Theo on a short leash."

At first Bernard wanted to respond negatively, that he had noticed nothing of the sort, but, as he was about to respond, the image of her squeezing close to Theo by the fire came to mind. He had an odd sensation at the time that it was territorial, and now it made sense.

"I noticed nothing out of the ordinary," he said evasively and diplomatically.

"Well, Theo is quite handsome. Maybe people are just projecting."

Bernard didn't know how to respond. He grabbed the beer and took a large sip, and noted, "Jules is very attractive. She has nothing to worry about."

"If you like the French," Hans laughed contemptuously.

Bernard thought to himself that he did like the French – who didn't? The image of Jules leaning over the table in her low-cut sweater came to mind. He recalled the soft olive skin of her neck and her sensual nose and lips. "She's very charming and accomplished."

"Hmm, yes. As you say, probably nothing to worry about. Are you going to see them again?"

"We didn't make any plans. It was a chance encounter. Who knows, we might run into each other again."

"Grindelwald is smaller than you think," Hans winked.

The sky was clearing, and Bernard was eager to get back on the slopes. He offered to pay, but Hans had already taken care of things when he had gone to the bathroom earlier.

"That's very generous of you. Thanks."

"My pleasure. I hope you enjoy your stay in Switzerland. Tell your friends about us!"

"What is this – a promotional advertisement for skiing in Switzerland?"

"It's all part of the strategic government relations outreach."

"Tell Theo hello for me if you see him. What a small world."

"I will – and *bisous* to Jules if you run into them again.

Bernard grabbed his skis, stepped into the bindings, and headed down the slope. Hans was already disappearing in the distance. He was a fast skier. Bernard took his time. The clouds were thinning, and the sun peeked through from time to time, casting long shadows across the trails. As he continued farther down the mountain, trails passed summer barns and huts closed for the winter. They were buried in a thick blanket of snow, only the eaves showing above the drifts. He paused to take in the view, glancing up at the terrain he had covered and looked down at the path before him. He inched forward and continued his descent.

In town, he stopped at the market to pick up some provisions before heading home. He had a craving for pasta, so he picked up vegetables, cheese, sauce, and spaghetti. The store had a generous selection of wine, so he selected a few bottles. The walk home was thankfully short. He hadn't anticipated the challenge of carrying home groceries with a pair of skis and walking in ski boots.

He undressed and took a nice, hot shower. The image of the youthful athletic skiers at the lift haunted him, a sense of his own youth fading. He leaned close to the mirror and ran the towel over his head, using his fingers to comb his hair into place. He kept his hair short and liked that it had remained dark, only a few errant strands of gray. He stepped back and ran the towel over abdomen and down his legs. He had been doing special training for the trip, so it pleased him to see more definition in his thighs and calves. He hung the towel on a rack and went into the bedroom. He grabbed a pair of shorts and jeans, slid them on, and stretched a long-sleeved tee-shirt over his head, walking barefoot into the kitchen.

A text popped up on his phone from one of his colleagues at the university. "Bernard, we need your help. One of the new recruiters is ill, and we were scheduled to be in Milan next week. Any chance you might be able to join me there? It's not far from where you are now, right?"

Robert was someone he had brought onto the team a few years ago - young, ambitious, and mercurial. He looked up to Bernard – as if he were a mentor, often confiding personal information. He went through a series of complicated relationships with women on a dating app. Bernard always wondered if he was gay, and the invitation to meet up in Milan alarmed him. He was fond of Robert, but he always felt he had to be on guard, keeping physical and emotional boundaries that Robert seemed eager to transgress.

He texted back, "Good to hear from you, Robert. Sorry I can't get away. Hope you can find someone else on staff."

Bernard chopped vegetables and cooked them in oil, stirring in tomatoes, sauce, and spices. He dropped a handful of spaghetti into the boiling water and waited for it to be ready.

A new text came in. "Okay, Bernard. Thanks anyway. By the way, I ran into someone called Alan, an archaeologist. Says he knows you. Seemed very interested in knowing where you were. He was asking for you."

Bernard wasn't sure how to respond. He typed, "He's a nice guy," then deleted it. He tried, "Yes, if you see him again, tell him hello for me," then deleted that as well. He settled with, "We met a long time ago. I'm surprised he remembers me."

The pasta was ready. Bernard strained the noodles and tossed them in the pan of sauce, emptying the mixture into a large ceramic bowl. He sprinkled on some cheese, poured a generous glass of wine, and began to enjoy the rich flavors of his dinner.

Bernard thought about Robert's texts and felt uneasy. While he had dismissed Alan long ago, and always maintained boundaries with Robert, he felt he was in a different place. Robert's texts had elicited a latent curiosity, a desire to see what had happened to Alan. He typed his name into a browser and scrolled through dozens of links to his work. He clicked on one of them and a photo of Alan at a dig in Israel filled the screen. Bernard chuckled at how he had aged. The shorts and baseball cap couldn't mask how the years had taken their toll on the handsome man he met many years ago in Cambridge. He had his arms slung over a young man's shoulder, undoubtedly a student or fellow archaeologist. He scrolled down and read about Alan's accomplishments and discoveries. He explored some social media posts and clicked on a link about personal information. It said he was single.

Bernard felt embarrassed, as if his clicks might be traced, that Alan or someone else might detect he was searching. It felt like trespassing, a curiosity more personal than professional, an attempt to satisfy a latent question, a 'what if.' He was relieved Alan had aged poorly, confirmation that he had made a good choice in marrying Susan, but he was still unsettled, restless, curious. He paused and hesitated, struggling with conflicting emotions of shame and desire, fear and daring – and then he typed into a new internet search, 'Theo Decker.'

3

Chapter Three

It was Saturday morning, and Bernard decided to ski one of the other major areas of the region called First. The base station for the gondola was just a few hundred meters from his apartment. He arrived just as it opened and hopped into a cabin filled with a group of teens, texting their friends, and exchanging comments in local dialect. He imagined his daughter, just a little older, laughing and playing with them. He missed her and couldn't wait for her visit. Maybe she would meet a nice Swiss guy.

He sized up the teens who, although wearing scuffed up pants, jackets, and helmets, were undoubtedly children of privilege. They made every effort to look middle class but had expensive phone devices, season passes to the lifts, referred to professors at their private schools in Bern and Basel, and were already talking about dinner at high-end restaurants in town. Bernard wasn't fluent in Swiss German, but could make out a phrase or two and pretended to check emails and texts on his device so he could listen unnoticed.

Two were brother and sister, perhaps twins. They looked alike and were roughly the same age. They seemed to have a unique bond, certainly stronger than ordinary siblings. One guy, Georg – a wiry athletic type - seemed hooked on Sam, that is Samantha. But he also spent inordinate energy trying to impress Marc. Marc sat leaning against the outside wall of the gondola. There was an air of aloofness as he stared at the scenery passing by with little regard for the jostling inside. He had pulled a stylish scarf halfway up his face, concealing an occasional furtive glance toward Georg. He had dark, wavy hair, a long neck, and a lanky torso. Bernard wondered if he was more self-conscious or guarded than aloof, doubting his own allure. Bernard chuckled as he thought of his own awkward adolescent years, recognizing himself in the enigmatic boy, looking out the window and secretly waiting for a glance or a sign from someone he admired.

The ride was breathtaking. The lift skimmed the top of pine forests perched over a deep valley with views of the towering peaks on the other side of a deep valley. It passed several midway stations before arriving at the terminus named First. From First, one could take another lift to Oberjoch. At 2500+ meters, the run all the way back to Grindelwald was an impressive 5000 foot vertical.

Bernard grabbed one of the first chairs to Oberjoch, where high above the tree line, the entire Jungfrau region was in plain sight. He paused and took in the magnificent views, feeling vertigo from the high vantage point. The beginning of the ski trail was broad and gentle, but Bernard tightened up as he noticed a ridge in the near distance, a sign of a sharp drop off. As he approached, his turns became uncertain, tentative. He skidded to a stop and looked down. "It doesn't look too bad," he tried to convince himself. He pushed off, made one turn, and then another. He leaned downhill and felt the edges of his skis grip the surface. The slope finally gave way to a series of more gentle hills before dumping people back at the base of the lift. He glanced up at what he had traversed and felt encouraged.

He made several more runs on Oberjoch before deciding to take a series of runs to Bort, an upscale lodge and restaurant half-way down the mountain. He slipped into the First station to use the bathroom and, when he came out, he heard someone yell, "Zoe!"

He looked for a little pink jacket but saw nothing. He thought he saw a dark black and red jacket, Theo's, drop below the sight line of the slope heading down the mountain. He quickly stepped into his skis, adjusted his goggles, and headed in the same direction. He arrived at a lower lift station and watched people load onto the chairs, but no Zoe, Theo, or Jules. He rode the lift back to the top and then skied down to Bort.

The classic Swiss lodge, nestled at the edge of a forest along a steep ski trail, had unobstructed views of the surrounding mountains, with Kleine Scheidegg gleaming in the far distance. Bernard unlatched his skis, leaned them against a rack, and walked onto the dining terrace. Most of the tables were already full or reserved. A small single table was free. Removing his helmet, gloves, and jacket, he took a seat and felt the warmth of the sun on his face.

The wait staff were darting about, taking orders, bringing out bottles of chilled white wine, and attending to the needs of the well-heeled crowd. There were few children, mostly couples and groups of friends – a handsome crowd, undoubtedly politicians and lobbyists from Bern. He listened in on nearby conversations, disputes about an upcoming conference on European collaboration, consternation about China's continued rise in power, and rumors of upcoming American elections. At one table, the conversation digressed to reviews of a new restaurant in town and regrets about the absence of any significant visual arts or galleries.

Bernard enjoyed the solitude and anonymity of his current circumstances, but wished he could share the moment with someone.

He and Susan had enjoyed a pleasant lunch there years ago. The memories were bittersweet. He hoped to bring Angela when she visited. He glanced around to see if he might spot Theo and Jules, but saw no one.

Nearby, under the eaves of the wooden structure, a row of old leathery men smoked cigarettes and nursed tall glasses of beer on a long bench. They were mostly silent, old friends just hanging out together. One made a comment, pointing toward a distant table. His companion nodded and then took a drag of his cigarette. *Celibataires* – singles - they were - he was, he thought to himself. How close was he to sharing their world, one cast off, adrift, without compass – just passing time?

Bernard pulled out his phone, checked emails, and read the latest news. After a couple of glasses of wine and a schnitzel with *frites*, he wasn't sure how much more skiing he had in him for the day. He hoped the profiteroles and espresso he had for dessert would kick in, and he'd get a second wind. He paid his tab and was walking to the ski rack when, out of the corner of his eyes, he spotted Jules. She was adjusting her scarf and waiting for the maître d' to find a table. He walked over to her.

"Jules!"

She turned and, with great fanfare, yelled, "Bernard! *Que Plaisir!*" They kissed each other on the cheeks. "Theo will be so excited to know you are here. He's in the bathroom."

"What a coincidence. Did you just get here?" She placed her hand over his forearm affectionately.

"No, actually, I just finished lunch. I'm trying to decide how much skiing I have left in me for the day."

At that point, Theo and Zoe came forward. Theo beamed when he saw Bernard and gave him a warm, affectionate hug. Bernard bent down to give Zoe a kiss on her cheek. "I was wondering if I might run into you sometime. How have you been doing?"

"I'm fine, thank you," Zoe said cheerfully.

"I see you have a new coat."

"It's the same color – but new."

"I like it. It looks good on you!"

Zoe pirouetted in place.

The maître d' let them know their table was ready. "Would you like to join us? I'm sure they can make another place," Theo offered, his hand placed warmly on Bernard's shoulder.

"No, thanks. I just finished. But I was wondering if you might like to come to my place for dinner. Are you free this evening?"

Theo and Jules looked at each other. She said, "No plans that we couldn't change for a dinner with our American friend. When would you like us to meet up?"

"Say about 6:30, maybe even 6:00. Timing is flexible. I was going to make an American dish – chili. It's nothing special but is a favorite ski dish back home."

"Sounds perfect. We'll see you later."

Theo put his arms around Jules's shoulder, and they headed to their table. Bernard walked over to the ski station, boarded the gondola, and rode to Schreckfeld, where he began a long run home.

He was delighted to have run into the Deckers. Jules seemed more friendly than he had expected, dropping the short leash she had Theo on the other night and being quite affectionate toward him, Bernard. Recalling Hans's comment the day before, he wondered if there were two Jules – the one who carefully guarded Theo and the other, an affable and beautiful young woman who could light up a room.

Bernard dropped off his skis and went to the market to get some appetizers and ingredients for the chili. He had begun to use vegetarian meat that had the same texture and flavor as beef, but none of the health or environmental demerits. His recipe included onions, peppers, stewed tomatoes, tomato paste, and a mixture of spices which, in Switzerland, he would have to improvise.

The Deckers arrived shortly after 6:30 with wine, flowers, and chocolate in hand. "Let me take your coats," he offered as they shook a few light snowflakes off onto the foyer floor.

"This is for you," Zoe said as she handed Bernard a bouquet of flowers.

"I'll find a vase right away. They are beautiful." Zoe beamed with delight and ran her hands along the wall, looking at the art hanging above her.

"And here's some wine and chocolate," Jules offered, giving Bernard a kiss on both cheeks. Theo shook his hand warmly and walked boldly into the living room.

"What a beautiful place. How did you find this?" Theo inquired, admiring the large glass window, balcony, and the warm fireplace.

"Just online. I guess I lucked out. I'm happy with it, and the location is excellent."

He invited them to sit and asked them what they wanted to drink. Cheese and hummus were already set out on the coffee table.

"What a coincidence to run into you today," Jules began, reaching over to cut a slice of cheese, her sweater sliding slightly down her soft shoulders and a dangling gold pendant drawing attention to her breasts hidden in the loose folds. Bernard stared until he thought she or Theo might notice.

"Yes indeed," Bernard stated, as if he had not hoped to run into them.

"And your week – all good?" Theo inquired.

"Yes, it's been quite nice. When did you come in from the city?"

"We came yesterday afternoon. My work was crazy," Jules noted.

"How long are you here?"

"Just until Sunday evening, I'm afraid," Theo explained. "There's a meeting in congress on Monday I have to attend." He took a long drink from his glass, placed it on the table, and gave Bernard a long look before reaching for a chip and dipping it into the hummus.

"Well, hopefully the conditions will be good tomorrow."

"They look like they will be superb," Jules remarked with a long ending to superb. Bernard was still infatuated with her accent and luscious pursed lips.

Theo wasn't as relaxed or at ease with himself as he had been the week before. Bernard thought he was anxious, preoccupied, a bit fidgety. He kept staring into his wineglass, tilting it back and forth as if deep in thought.

After appetizers, Bernard invited them to the table, where he set out a large dish of chili and a smaller one with pasta. He had warmed a fresh baguette in the oven and served it on a cutting board. "Save room for apple pie!" he added.

Zoe's eyes widened.

Initially Bernard was going to bring up the fact that he met Hans earlier in the week, but thought it might be best to avoid it, particularly since he had made comments about Jules.

They discussed the latest news - decisions the US made to invest in Latin America, an arguably better approach to immigration than building more walls and surveillance. The Europeans had done the same to deal with immigrants from Africa and the Middle East, and it had worked well. Theo had been involved in those decisions and supported what the US wanted to do in their own hemisphere.

Theo leaned back slightly, his well-developed chest pushing against the tight-fitting dark knit sweater. He creased his broad forehead, showing interest in the subtleties of the conversation. His hazel eyes sparkled, and Bernard felt their intensity as he spoke.

"You never told us where you were from," Theo inquired. "Are you from Boston itself?"

"I grew up just south of the city in a small coastal town, Hingham."

"And college?"

"Undergraduate at Yale and graduate at Harvard."

"Wow, quite the pedigree." Theo raised his eyebrows.

Bernard blushed and added, "I was lucky to have a father in higher education who pulled a few strings."

"Are your parents still alive?" Jules inquired, leaning attentively toward him.

"No, they have both passed. And you – that is, and your parents?" he said, giving them each a look.

"Mine are still alive. They live in a small town near Luzern," Theo noted.

"And Jules's parents - are they in France and Geneva?" Bernard asked.

Jules perked up and said, "They go back and forth between Lyon and Geneva."

"So, I assume Zoe speaks French, German, Swiss German, and some English?" he asked, looking over at Zoe, who was beaming.

"Yes, she's very gifted in that way."

"So, you're here for two months?" Theo inquired.

"Yes, that's the plan. My friends thought I was crazy to go away so long, but I don't have any responsibilities at the moment, and it seemed like a good idea."

"I'm sure it will be a good time to think and decide what you'd like to do next."

"That's what I'm hoping – as well as to ski as much as I can!"

Theo proposed a toast to skiing and new friends. They all raised and clinked their glasses and continued with the chili.

Jules paid more attention to Zoe, and Theo continued his barrage of questions, asking more and more personal ones, sliding his chair closer to Bernard's.

"How's it been since your divorce? Are you dating? Anyone of interest? Sorry if I'm asking too many personal questions."

"No, I've been just trying to organize practical things. Plus, it's a little daunting these days with dating apps, profiles, and all the other things one has to do to meet people."

"I know. I feel fortunate Jules and I met in college." He looked over at her affectionately, then turned toward Bernard. Bernard felt his intense gaze.

Bernard asked, "Did you date anyone before Jules?"

Theo looked away evasively. "No, not really. And you?"

"The same." Both looked down at the table, fingers nervously tapping the surface.

"I don't know what I would do without her. She and Zoe are my world."

"They're both great. You're lucky!"

"What will happen with your daughter? That must be tough," Theo inquired thoughtfully.

"She's moved in with her mother but is in college. She's coming next week for a visit."

"Well, I hope we might have a chance to meet her."

Bernard was struck by the implication that there would be another rendezvous. "That would be nice. Maybe we can meet on the slope some afternoon."

"Or we can have you over again. I can invite some friends who have children of the same age. She can meet them."

"I'm sure she would enjoy that."

Everyone finished their chili, and Bernard served slices of apple pie and ice cream afterwards. Later, Jules stood up and mentioned softly that she was going to take Zoe to the bathroom. "It's just down the hall," Bernard noted.

Theo leaned over, resting his shoulder on Bernard's and, in a low voice, said, "I am going to tell you something that is strictly confidential. I was curious about you and your wife, and I looked you up in our classified system. Aside from general information on the internet about your job, there wasn't much else. But I found a lot of information about your wife. Would you like to come to Bern someday? I have some information you might find interesting."

Bernard pulled back, intrigued, and asked, "What kind of information?"

"It's rather sensitive, classified. Can you come on Tuesday? My calendar is relatively clear."

"Sure," Bernard said hesitantly, with alarm. "Where do I find you?"

"Let's meet at a restaurant. Security at my office is complicated. Plus, there's the risk of surveillance. I know a discrete brasserie."

Theo scribbled a name and address on the back of his business card and handed it quickly to Bernard as Jules's footsteps resounded down the wooden hallway.

She didn't sit, indicating it was time for them to go. Theo stood up, holding Bernard's inquisitive stare for an uncomfortable length of time. Jules didn't seem to pay attention, helping Zoe with her jacket.

They all exchanged warm embraces and kisses. "The chili was delicious. Thanks for sharing your warm hospitality with us. We're so glad to have gotten to know you," Jules said affectionately.

Theo nodded assent, buttoning up his jacket and slipping on his gloves. "*Schüss*," he said as he gave Bernard a warm embrace just before exiting and waving from the top of the stairs.

Bernard cleared the table and did dishes. He settled afterwards into a large comfortable chair in front of the fireplace and racked his brain, trying to guess what Theo might have to share about Susan. Did her work at the aerospace company have some nefarious aspects to it? Was she in some trouble? There was a part of him that hoped she was. He felt blindsided and angry by her abrupt decision to divorce and quickly remarry. She denied that she and Charles had been having an affair, but he had a difficult time believing her.

He kept reminding himself that people get divorced all the time. They were an exception, in fact - a rare intact family. Most of Angela's friends lived in blended families, children shuttled between father, mother, and stepparents. He and Susan prided themselves in having minimal conflict, sharing power in the relationship, and embracing non-traditional gender roles, Bernard often taking care of domestic chores and Susan bringing in a bigger salary and over-seeing finances.

Angela had already set him up on a dating app, but he found the entire process discouraging. He preferred the old-fashioned way of meeting people in social gatherings, picking up on subtle vibes and chemistry. Alas, bars were more depressing, filled with 20-year-olds and the occasional age-appropriate person who looked tired and overly lubricated with booze and recreational drugs.

Theo and Jules seemed so cute together, her feminine sensuality complementing his more cerebral nature. He was brooding; she was effervescent. He was hard, she soft. Theo filled a room with a raw manly presence, she with a beguiling grace and charm.

Had either been involved in an indiscretion, an infidelity, even if only imagined or entertained. Don't we all imagine what our lives would be like with someone else, a person whose faults are un-known and whose assets are all too apparent? What would happen to Zoe if they ever divorced? What a tragic breach for an innocent young girl?

Bernard reprimanded himself for his mental excursion and returned to the original question. What did Theo have to share with him? What confidence or secret did he hold, eager to unload? What motivated his interest, intrigue, and curiosity – a curiosity strong enough to have looked them both up on a classified system? Bernard felt exposed but excited to find out Susan's secrets, to gain leverage and power when he had been rendered so powerless. Yes, he too had been curious, had looked Theo up, but found little that he didn't already know.

He turned off the lights, went into the bedroom, jumped in under the cold down comforter, and felt its snug embrace. He closed his eyes, but his mind raced. It would be a sleepless right.

4

Chapter Four

On Tuesday, Bernard took an early train to Bern, giving him time to explore the old town before lunch. The train curved through a deep canyon, passing back and forth over a stream parallel to a roadway. Small patches of farmland were covered in snow, tool sheds and barns sitting idly by. Tall fir trees hung tenaciously to rocky overhangs. He strained his head upward to catch fleeting glimpses of bright snow fields thousands of feet above the gorge through which he passed. The train was relatively empty at the early hour, except for a few intrepid skiers making an early trek to Mürren.

At Interlaken, Bernard changed trains, boarding a commuter line between Bern, Thun, and Interlaken. Riders ranged from posh skiers heading back to larger cities, students heading to classes, workers on their way to jobs, and retired people looking for something to do. An older white-haired woman sat cross-armed next to a window, begrudgingly nodding to an older man who tipped his hat to her as he boarded in Thun. Teens gathered in a pack, texting friends and hanging on to each other. Bernard enjoyed the anonymity of looking like neither a tourist nor a worker. Several passengers eyed him suspiciously, trying to figure him out – a foreigner who looked at home.

Bernard had always fantasized about being a spy, riding trains between European capitals and passing coded information to secret contacts. Most Americans flocked to the Continent to see monuments and museums, relying on the ubiquity of English to facilitate their journeys. Bernard relished fitting in, speaking local languages, and going about everyday activities as if he were a native.

His love of languages was first sparked by the occasional trip to the North End of Boston where the Italian community settled. He loved hearing the servers and cooks speaking to each other in Italian and the old men on the street at the cafes playing cards, drinking grappa, and conversing in local dialect.

One year, his family went to Quebec to ski. He still remembered the charming girl on the lift with him, speaking to her friend in French. It was at that point he resolved to decipher foreign languages in order to bridge cultural and linguistic barriers, to become a citizen of the world.

The train pulled into Bern, where people jumped out of the door, eager to make connections to other trains or make their way to homes and offices. Bernard joined the wave of people and exited the station onto a vast plaza with trams, cafes, and large stores. He had always been curious about historic Bern, so he took one of the smaller roads off the square and followed it down the slope of the city. A scramble of streets gave way to several well-maintained medieval lanes lined with covered walkways where boutiques, galleries, and restaurants beckoned locals and tourists.

As capital of Switzerland, Bern seemed more like a quaint medieval town than a political center. Swiss politics was still provincial and built on long-term relationships and traditions. Bernard imagined that for centuries little had changed under these arcades – the same routines, purchases, vendors, and pace of life. In every window, goods were strategically placed and labeled. No one seemed in a hurry. Everyone was courteous, graceful, and impeccably dressed.

Hoping to find a gift for Angela, he pushed open the door of a shop specializing in crystals. In the display window there were glass bowls filled with colorful raw chunks of amethyst, rose quartz, blue azurite, and green aventurine. A young 30-something-year-old man greeted him warmly. He had fully expected a woman, one of those new age mystical sorcerer types. Instead, a slightly tan, athletic man speaking in a deep melodious voice offered to help. He was busy wrapping several pieces of black tourmaline in copper wire to be used as pendants. Bernard already knew they absorbed unhelpful energy, having watched his Italian grandmother wear crystals and place them strategically around the house to create the right vibe. Whenever she faced a problem, she created a grid of crystals and wrote her imagined outcome on a piece of paper, laying it under the gems.

Bernard spotted a large cluster of clear quartz found near Grindelwald to give to his daughter. As he was being rung up by the shop owner, he glanced over his shoulder and noticed beautiful patterns of minerals that had been artfully placed in framed mats, small but dazzling pieces of stone linked by delicate threads in a geometric design. The shop owner caught Bernard's gaze and said, "They're beautiful, aren't they?"

"Extremely. I've never seen anything like them."

"A local artist produces them for us. She has a gift for assembling the right stones into an energetic pattern. I know some people don't buy into that, but I can't tell you how many people come back to the shop to report how powerful they are."

"Can I see that one?" Bernard asked, pointing to one of them.

"Ah, I can see why that caught your eye. It is called 'Le Travers.' I think in English it means a crossing or movement beyond a boundary or line. It is for those facing limits or challenges and unleashes the power to unbind oneself and cross onto a new path. Here, take it as a gift."

"I couldn't. I'm just getting this crystal for my daughter."

"That's what you thought." He winked at Bernard. "You can return the favor later."

Reluctantly, Bernard accepted the shopkeeper's generosity. He wrapped both items in beautiful paper and placed them in a small bag with handles.

Bernard stepped back outside and continued to stroll under the arcade. He entered the front door of a small men's boutique, lured in by several colorful sweaters in the window. An older man nodded from behind the counter, continuing to fold some shirts. Bernard walked over to a rack and flipped through several items, looking for his size. He found a nice zippered sports sweater. He pulled off his jacket and tried it on as the shopkeeper glanced over at him. Standing in front of the mirror, Bernard turned from side to side, noting how nice it fell on his hips. The color was rich and complemented his complexion, and the cut showcased his broad shoulders. The shopkeeper beamed in approval and gently spoke across the space. "It looks very nice on you. Would you like to get it?"

"Yes, please."

"Do you want to wear it?"

Bernard nodded. The shopkeeper cut the tags off and handed it to him. Bernard slipped it on, zipped it part way up, and then put his jacket on over the sweater.

"Where are you from?"

"Boston."

"We don't see too many people from Boston here – or even from the States. Most are off skiing."

"I am, but I came into town for a meeting."

"Well, you'll look good for the meeting."

Bernard smiled, paid the bill, and bowed to the shopkeeper, who winked at him. He then went out into the arcade, followed it to the end, and then began making his way back toward the government side of town. He checked the address and found the brasserie for his *rendezvous* with Theo. He opened a large wooden door where an austere but helpful maître d' greeted him. "*Gruezi. Wie viel sind Sie?*

Bernard explained that he was alone, meeting someone. He looked over the tables and saw Theo waving at him. The maitre d' accompanied him to Theo's table and took his coat. Theo shook his hand warmly and invited him to sit. They were in a private booth, toward the back of a spacious classic French-style room with dark wood paneling and a white mosaic tile floor.

Theo returned to his seat, leaned his elbows on the table, and wrung his hands nervously. "I'm having a beer. Can I offer you something?"

"I'll have some wine." Theo waved the server over and ordered for him. Bernard felt himself trembling a bit, a rush of adrenaline as if waiting for the results of a tough exam.

Bernard was used to seeing Theo in casual clothes. In jacket and tie, he looked older, traditional, but also handsome and distinguished. He was tempted to make a comment, but feared Theo might take it as too intimate, familiar. It surprised him when Theo asked, "Is that a new sweater? It looks very nice on you."

"Yes, just picked it up at a little boutique in town. I didn't realize Bern was so charming. I thought it would have been more of a boring capital city."

"We're a lot more interesting than we look," Theo saying with a grin.

"You mean there's more than meets the eye?" Bernard retorted, wishing he could have taken back the suggestive statement he made so spontaneously. He wasn't sure where it had come from and was worried it would offend Theo.

Thankfully, the glass of wine arrived. He toasted Theo and took a long sip and perused the menu evasively. "What do you recommend?"

"It's classic brasserie fare – all quite good. If you like meat, the *steak-frites* or the *steak-au-poivre* are good. There are also salads and soup if you want something lighter.

"I'll do the *steak-frites*," Bernard decided with little deliberation.

"Me, too. Good choice." Theo added.

Theo looked at him warmly, and Bernard felt like he was with an old friend, catching up. He had to keep reminding himself that he had only met him recently and had only been with him a few times.

"So, your trip in was good?"

"Yes, it was easy. It was actually good to take a break from skiing."

Theo began tapping his fingers nervously on the table. "Well, I'm sure you are eager to know what I have to share." Clearing his throat, he continued, "I was curious about you last week, about the work you do. We're always on the lookout for people we might partner with in the States. I looked you up. I found the information about your job at the university. But in our system, I found references to your wife." He paused nervously. "What kind of work does she do?"

"She's an aerospace executive and sales rep."

"Hmm." Theo murmured. "Did she ever talk about any work with the US government?"

"She and her company have a lot of government contracts. Occasionally she mentioned them, particularly when she had to fly overseas to smooth things over."

"Did she ever mention that she worked directly for the government - in the area of intelligence?"

"You mean as a spy?"

Theo took another sip of his beer. The server came with their plates. Once he left and had gotten far enough away from the table, Theo answered, "Yes, as a spy."

Bernard turned red and leaned forward over the table. "What do you know?"

"The more troublesome question is, what do you know?" Theo whispered.

"I know nothing. Yes, she did some classified work, but it was in international sales."

"That's not exactly the case. She's listed as an agent for US intelligence. What's curious is that one of her primary duties," he began tentatively, wringing his hands more nervously, "is monitoring you."

"Me?" Bernard exclaimed, shocked, leaning back in his chair.

"Yes, you. That's why I thought you probably knew nothing about her or her work."

"Why would the US government want to monitor me?"

"That's a good question. They could have worried that with your foreign student contacts and travel, another country might recruit you. Or, more likely the case, some of the students and their families are assets for other governments and agencies, and they wanted to keep a close eye on them through you."

"Oh my God, the thought of working for another government never crossed my mind."

"They don't know that, and someone could always approach you. And, if your wife had been able to get into your computer system – which she probably did - the US government would have had access to all sorts of Middle Eastern recruits, their families, and personal information submitted in applications. It would be a treasure trove of information obtained without putting other assets at risk."

Bernard became quiet, stunned by the news. He wracked his brain, thinking back at situations he may have overlooked. Was he that naïve? Bernard pushed the food around on his plate and looked up at Theo. "Are you sure about this? Why would all of this be in a dossier?"

"Even though Switzerland is neutral, it is friendly with US

intelligence. There's a mutual respect and reciprocity about keeping each other informed of activity – although much of it is a façade to impress each other that we are being transparent. Susan is not a high security agent, so her information and activity are reported, even if classified."

"Could you get in trouble for sharing this with me?"

"Potentially, although this is hardly an internationally delicate matter. Some of the other things she does, if I knew what they were, might be."

"Maybe this explains the extra scrutiny I get at passport controls around the world."

"It could, although with your extensive travel and type of work, it might just be extra precautions."

"So now that we are divorced?"

"Ah, an interesting matter," Theo interjected, looking evasively in the distance. "It would appear she has new responsibilities."

Bernard was now piecing things together. He lost his job, she divorced him, she married Charles, an international political scientist. Perhaps he was her new work.

"So, our marriage. A sham," he said dejectedly.

"I'm not sure I know what the word sham means."

"Unreal, a façade, a pretext for something else."

Bernard felt the feeling vanish from his extremities, almost as if he had left his body. He gripped his fork, trying to remain anchored to the moment. Theo reached over, placed his hand on Bernard's, and inquired, "Are you okay?"

"Yeah, yeah, I'm okay." But he wasn't. He glanced down the aisle of the restaurant, counting the number of lamps at the end of each booth and noting the themes of French posters decorating the back wall. He couldn't look Theo in the eyes. He felt embarrassed.

Theo hadn't removed his hand yet, and Bernard felt self-conscious about the gesture.

"Bernard," Theo continued, "I'm here for you."

Bernard thought the comment odd and pulled his hand out from under Theo's. "What do you mean?"

Theo leaned back, removed his hands from the table, and let them rest in his lap. "Maybe I shouldn't have shared this with you." He apologized.

"No, I'm glad you did, although the whole thing is surreal."

"Perhaps it wasn't my place."

"Whose place would it have been to tell me? I'm angry – at Susan – at my government." Bernard's emotional volatility erupted.

"You have every right to be. It's a betrayal."

"How could someone pretend to be in love for 20 years? How could I be in a relationship that was a lie all that time?"

Theo shook his head, not sure what kind of words could offer any consolation. He stared at Bernard, who evaded his glance.

Bernard remained silent. He didn't touch his food but kept emptying his glass of wine. Theo was at a loss for what to do. In solidarity, he didn't eat. The server asked if there was something wrong, and both shook their heads no. He offered his assistance if they needed anything.

"I'll have a coffee," Bernard noted. "And a brandy."

"Me, too," Theo added to the server.

Bernard regained feeling in his legs, and the brandy helped him relax.

"All those years," he mused. "No wonder things changed so suddenly."

Theo was curious, but worried about meddling. "Where there any signs?"

"Not that I noticed. But, in retrospect, yes."

"Like what?"

"Things were a little too regimented and scheduled. There wasn't any spontaneity or playfulness."

Theo asked timidly, "You mean around sex?"

Embarrassed, Bernard answered, "Yes – around sex. It was good, but not great. Regular but not frequent – and certainly never creative."

As a politician, Theo read people quickly. When he first met Bernard at the clinic, he was distracted by his slim physique and impeccable outfit. He thought he was another pretentious and privileged American. But the solicitous care of Zoe and his affable and unassuming demeanor quickly changed his opinion. Even Jules, ever difficult to impress, found him alluring. Zoe, sensitive and thoughtful, took to him right away. Bernard's enthusiasm for life and adventure, exploring other lands and cultures, was contagious. It pained Theo to see that spark fade so quickly with the information he had just delivered. He wanted to console him, to reach over and give him a big hug, but he held back. He watched Bernard's eyes glass over and lose their intensity.

"Bernard, let's take a walk." Theo signaled to the server to retrieve their coats and bring the check. Attentively, the server took care of them right away.

The bright sunshine and cool air were invigorating. Bernard launched into an unexpected tirade. "That filthy piece of shit! All of those years lost to an unfeeling, manipulative ice princess."

Theo stepped back, spreading his arms wide, not expecting the outburst. "You have every right to feel that way! I'd be – what do you say in English – raging mad!"

"I am. I can't believe it. It even makes me question my own feelings. How could I have missed this? Am I so naïve?"

"She's a professional, Bernard. And she probably had feelings for you. How could she not have developed an affection for you – even some degree of friendship? It's inevitable."

Bernard thought back to the fun times they had and had to admit to himself that there must have been something between them. They had good conversations, a shared sense of the world, and partnered well in raising Angela. Susan was either a master at deception or must have had some affection for him – fussing over his attire and always noting how graceful he was aging. She was always saying to him, "You look so much younger than your colleagues who don't seem to be aging too well – my handsome scholar." Her compliments made him feel special, loved, confident.

They walked past a small pub, and Theo invited Bernard in for a drink. "Why not?" Bernard replied to the offer. "It's going to take a lot of alcohol to deal with this."

"Finally, a little humor."

Bernard smiled. "But she's still a piece of shit!"

"Yes, she is," Theo added. "Now, let's have a drink."

The room was uncharacteristically busy, with tables crowded and only a few seats free at the bar. They grabbed two stools squeezed between business executives having a late lunch. Bernard felt less self-conscious. No one could overhear them with all the noise. They ordered two scotches. Theo faced him, one hand placed warmly on Bernard's knee. Bernard began, "How do you really know if it is real – I mean – 20 years later you think you are in a loving, successful, relatively conflict-free relationship and boom – she's gone? How can that be?"

"We all imagine or create the reality we want to see. Unless we are confronted with something traumatic or world-altering, things bumble along as we expect them."

"Oh, so you're a philosopher now."

"Not really – but think about it – unless we are confronted with something challenging, we stay in the comfortable rut we have created for ourselves."

"But I liked my comfortable rut! I had a good job, a good family, and a nice life."

Theo placed his drink on the bar and now, with both hands

holding Bernard's legs together affectionately, he looked at him intensely in the eyes and said solemnly, "And you will find something better."

Bernard felt comforted by Theo's gesture, strong, assuring, and supportive. But the intensity of Theo's eyes made him nervous. He looked off and then back again. "So, what about you? Are you in a comfortable rut or living the dream?"

Theo paused, raised his eyebrow, and replied, "If you only knew."

"Well, tell me – Mr. politician with a secure job, lovely wife, talented daughter, and a life most people in the world would envy – what do I not know?"

"Let's save it for another time. Today is about you, not me."

"So, there's another time?"

Theo grinned. "Of course. I've got to recruit you for the Swiss."

Bernard didn't know whether Theo was joking or serious. "I don't come cheap."

"I knew that the first day I met you."

Bernard took a long sip of scotch, hiding a grin.

"Are you okay?" Theo inquired warmly of Bernard, gazing into his eyes.

"Well, a little shocked, but feeling better now. Maybe the information helps put things into perspective and minimizes my sense of inadequacy."

"You should definitely not feel inadequate. You have so much going for you. Take advantage of the new freedom you have."

Bernard considered Theo's comment carefully and realized he had nothing to regret about himself and everything to look forward to.

They ordered a second round of scotches. Bernard had a moderate buzz going. He could usually hold his alcohol, but couldn't keep up with Theo. The bar emptied as people returned to work. Theo and Bernard claimed more space and turned toward the bar, where they leaned on the gray marble counter and nursed their drinks.

The bartender, wearing a classic white apron over black pants and shirt, dried glasses and listened discreetly to their conversation. Occasionally, he raised an eyebrow, undoubtedly alarmed by what he heard. He took care of other patrons at the bar, most calling him by his first name, Rudi. Rudi had a friendly smile and a handsome face and looked like he had a loyal following.

Theo looked at his watch and flagged Rudi for the check. "Hey, I'm sorry, I have a meeting in a half hour. I have to get back to the office. Are you going to be okay?"

Bernard didn't want the afternoon to end. Theo could see the disappointment on his face. "Why don't we make plans to continue this later?"

Bernard nodded.

"I'll walk you to the station." Theo offered. They paid their tab, put on their coats, and walked out into the shadowy light of late afternoon. They agreed upon a ski rendezvous the following weekend when Angela would be visiting from the States. Bernard and Theo embraced each other warmly, gave each other a kiss on the cheek, and Bernard hopped aboard the train.

It was getting dark, so Bernard could see little out of the windows. The news of Susan's work was confounding. What suspicions could the US government have had that would lead them to take such drastic action? He thought back, twenty years before. The political situation was different. Xenophobia was rampant, and hostility to immigration was a festering sore. Universities were accused of fostering a leftist socialist agenda, even partnering with European socialists. Of course, all of this was fake news and of no serious foundation, but bureaucrats were eager to show they were doing their part to reclaim an idealized past.

Bernard wondered if his wife was more conservative than she let on, all part of a façade. Maybe she was monitoring more than his recruits or liaisons - maybe his own political views were in question.

He now felt sorry for Charles and wondered if he should warn him. Who would believe him?

The afternoon with Theo had been interesting of its own accord. Theo's affection and familiarity surprised Bernard. He had pegged him as someone more reserved. He stroked the top of his hand, searching for the lingering warmth of Theo's touch. He rubbed his knees for the sensation of security he had when they had been held tightly in Theo's hands. Was all of that more than friendly affection?

It was dark outside, and he looked at his reflection in the glass, pushing a few stray locks of hair back into place and adjusting his scarf carefully around his neck. He doubted his own attractiveness and found Theo's attention confounding. Was he an unusually sensitive man, someone seeking to assure a friend during a time of crisis, or was something else happening, a dramatic shift of plot, a whole new narrative developing? The implications were too daunting to sort through at the hour, and the shocking revelations about Susan had drained him, so he closed his eyes, lulled to sleep with the gentle rocking of the carriage.

Bernard woke when the train whistled its arrival at the station in Grindelwald. He walked through the quiet darkness of the town and, once inside his apartment, decided to search the internet for information about Susan. He already was familiar with her social media presence but was curious to see what she posted on professional sites and what would come up online. A few links to her aerospace company popped up, including some critical articles about their support for right-wing governments. He wondered if she was involved in more than just a bit of surveillance and might be deep in international intrigue.

He scrolled through some photos on social media, pictures they had taken in Vermont skiing with colleagues of her from work. Who in the group might also be spies? He immediately thought of Frank, a human resource executive who traveled to their sites around the world and was always guarded, concealing his thoughts and evasive about plans. His wife Francis was a charming stay-at-home mom who volunteered at local charities and hovered over her kids. Suddenly, Bernard noticed a picture of a party at Frank's house, a gathering for their anniversary. The usual group of friends were there but, in the back of the yard, he noticed two men talking. Since this was a group of their closest friends, he thought it curious that there were two men who no one knew. At the time, it didn't strike him as anything other than a bit odd, strange. But now, he wondered if they were secret service or some security detail given the number of assets present.

He glanced back out of the window into the dark winter night and wondered what else he had missed and what kind of trouble he might face if anyone detected he was onto their secret.

5

Chapter Five

A few flakes of snow danced in the muted afternoon light as the train pulled into Grindelwald station with a sharp whistle. Bernard awaited enthusiastically for his daughter. Tourists poured out of the train cars, lugging suitcases and skis. Behind a large contingent of teens, Bernard spotted Angela's red ski jacket. He walked briskly toward her and caught her eye.

"Dad!" she screamed as she dropped her suitcase and reached her arms around him.

"Angela! I can't believe you're here!" Bernard leaned back, looking at his daughter and holding her shoulders warmly. She unzipped her jacket as she struggled to gather her belongings – her suitcase, ski bag, and ski boots.

"It's so good to see you." She kissed him on the cheeks. "I can see now why you love it here. It is breathtaking." She pivoted in place, taking in the bustle of activity, the Swiss-style chalets, and the fresh snow. Her blonde hair bounced on her shoulders, and her soft complexion glowed as she smiled warmly. Several young skiers noticed her, making not-so-concealed gestures of interest in the newly arrived American.

"How was your flight? Your train?"

"All good – uneventful. Although I had a little trouble at customs. They had a lot of questions."

Bernard raised his eyebrow but decided not to ask more.

"Let me carry your skis and boots. The apartment is just a short walk into town."

People were coming down from the slopes and gathering at bars for drinks, creating a crowded maze along the sidewalk. Angela tugged at her father's arm in front of a ski shop. "Oh my God, everything is so beautiful here."

He nodded and said, "We'll have to go shopping later. Looks like you need a new coat."

Angela smiled. As they continued to make their way, she looked back, having caught the eye of a cute ski instructor wearing a red jacket and pants. She sighed.

"You tired?" Bernard asked as he heard her sigh.

"No, just distracted."

"There's a lot of eye candy here," Bernard noted.

"Dad, I've never heard you use that language before. What's gotten into you?"

"Nothing, just stating facts. It's a beautiful place with a lot of handsome people."

They made their way up the hill, and Bernard unlocked the door, letting Angela into the apartment. Her eyes widened in amazement. "What a place. How did you find this?"

"I used a rental app. I guess I lucked out."

"I'd say you did. This is great. Mom would be so jealous if she knew."

"Let's keep her in the dark – at least for the time being."

"I'm so sorry. I didn't mean to stir things up," she said apologetically.

Bernard gave her a warm hug and said, "I'm just glad you're here. An entire week together. I hope you don't mind the sofa," Bernard said. "It's fold-out but has a nice mattress."

She nodded. As she opened the suitcase, Bernard pointed out a cabinet with some drawers and storage space. "This is all perfect. Thanks so much for having me."

"Are you kidding? By the way, how is your mom? Was she upset you were coming?"

"No, she seemed relieved I was getting away. She said to say hello. She's still very apologetic. Even though I said I always knew she would leave you, I never imagined it would be so sudden, and that she would hook up with someone like Charles. What a bore!"

"Yes, but he's an internationally renowned political scientist."

"What does that have to do with anything?"

"I don't know. Don't mind me. I'm still a little bitter." He had decided not to say anything – at least for the moment - about her mother's work, but he couldn't help throwing out a few bits of information here and there. "Are you excited to ski? This place is amazing."

"I told some of my friends at school. They were so jealous."

"Tomorrow we'll start early. I'll give you a tour of the area. On Saturday, we're going to join some friends I met."

Angela looked at her dad in amazement. "You made friends already? How is that possible?"

"What? You don't think I'm capable?"

"Of course, you're capable – it's just that mom was always the social one. You seemed to handle yourself well, but I never thought of you as the initiator. That's cool. Who are they?"

"It's a long story, but a couple's daughter got hurt on the

mountain, and I found her. We met at the clinic, and they invited me for dinner. They're a wonderful couple and family."

"Are they Swiss?"

"Yes. They live in Bern and have a house here."

"I look forward to meeting them."

"Why don't you change? We'll go out shopping and grab something to eat."

Angela went into the bathroom, took a shower, and came out into the living room in a pair of light blue thermal underwear, drying her hair with a towel. She cocked her head to the right and then to the left, a mannerism she picked up from her mother. Bernard stared at her in disbelief, feeling affection for Angela but waves of chagrin toward Susan.

"You okay, dad?"

"Yeah sure. I just miss you."

"I miss you, too."

Bernard smiled, gave his daughter another embrace, and said, "Let's get going. The shops close early."

Angela pulled on some jeans, a pullover, and wrapped a scarf around her neck. Bernard helped her with her jacket, and they headed out the door.

Bernard took her to Bruno's shop, a young man who had helped Bernard buy his own ski clothes and equipment a few weeks earlier. It was busy, but Bruno couldn't help fussing over Angela, darting briskly around the racks to find unique jackets and pants for her to try on. "This is perfect. It brings out your blue eyes and golden complexion.," he said as he held up a blue jacket in front of her.

Bernard stared him down. Angela tried on several outfits, posing in front of a generous full-length mirror in the middle of the shop. She settled on a pricy French jacket. Bernard gulped as he handed Bruno his credit card.

They strolled down the main street where a light snowfall

brightened the pavement. They slipped into a popular place for an espresso and a glass of wine. People squeezed tightly against a wooden bar and told stories of their day on the slopes. Bernard realized he was older than most but relished the attempts local young men were making to wrest Angela's attention away from him. Her eyes wandered, but she seemed eager to update him on Susan's comings and goings.

"She's different with Charles than she was with you. I'm not convinced she loves him," she noted.

"What do you mean?" Bernard pressed, suspecting he already knew the answer.

"Well, she seems less affectionate than she was with you. They go to a lot of faculty parties, and they host gatherings at Charles' house, but I don't sense any chemistry."

"You've mentioned a few times that you thought she would always leave me. Why do you say that?" Bernard inquired, taking a sip of his wine.

Angela looked off in the distance as if in thought and then turned to her dad and looked him in the eyes, "I'm not sure. As a kid, I felt that her work was her passion. She traveled a lot, and you and I were home alone. When she returned home, you lit up, but she seemed like she was already planning her next trip."

"Hmm," Bernard murmured in thought.

"Didn't you notice it?" Angela inquired.

"I just thought she was really busy. I felt sorry for her."

"But weren't there tensions?" she asked.

"Nothing more than what any other couple faces. I thought we were okay."

"So, you noticed nothing between her and Charles?"

"Nothing," Bernard said emphatically.

Angela had a look of realization – that they had somehow deceived her dad. A lonely tear ran down her cheek.

"Don't cry, dear. I'm fine." He rubbed his hands on her legs to assure her. He took the last sip of wine from his glass and set it on the bar. "Shall we go to dinner?"

Angela nodded, but she was glancing beyond Bernard to a young man standing with his friends at the corner of the bar.

"We can stay if you want," he added.

"No. I'm hungry. Let's go."

Bernard paid the tab, and they walked out into the cold air. They headed up the hill along the main road and settled on a charming Swiss restaurant for dinner. Inside, carved wooden booths were filled with couples enjoying fondue and drinks over candlelight. The maître d' set them at a table near a frosted window where colorful silhouettes passed back and forth outside in the increasingly intense snowfall.

They opened the menus, and Angela's eyes widened. "It's so expensive here."

"Yes, but the prices include tips. Think about home when you add 20% as a gratuity. You just add a little gesture of appreciation here."

"Still," Angela said, calculating in her mind the exchange rate from dollars to Swiss Francs.

"Don't worry. We're here on a vacation – so get what you'd like. And I know you will not order the filet."

"What do you think of the mushroom risotto with a nice salad?" she asked.

"For you or for me?"

"For me."

"Then I think it's fine. I'm going to get a schnitzel with *frites*."

"I can't believe you still eat that disgusting meat, dad!" she added emphatically.

"You'd be proud of me. I've cut back. I even made chili with vegetarian meat the other day."

She turned up her nose. "How did that turn out?"

"It was good. The problem was getting the right spices here."

The server came and took their orders and returned with a bottle of wine Bernard had selected. She opened it and poured some in each of their glasses. Angela raised her glass to her dad's and said, "Thanks for having me. It's good to be here with you."

"Thanks! I'm glad we have this time with each other. I miss you and hope you are okay."

"I'm fine. I just hope you're okay, dad!"

"I am," he said without elaboration.

"I can't believe you're here for a couple of months."

"It's a good break for me."

"You seem different," Angela noted, looking at her dad intensely. "More self-confident and alive."

"Must be the good mountain air and skiing."

"No, there's something else," as she stared into his eyes as if the pry some information out of him. He looked back stoically, and she asked excitedly, "Oh my God, did you meet someone?"

"No," he said emphatically.

"Well, you should. You're still young and handsome. You'd be a great catch."

"Thank you, dear, but I'm not sure I feel up to it at the moment. The pain from the divorce is still raw."

"I'm sure, but you need to move on."

"I have."

She took a long sip of her wine but kept her gaze glued to her father, trying to uncover whatever it was she had detected. It was an almost imperceptible change, but clearly something.

They enjoyed their dinner and wandered back to the apartment where Angela fell quickly asleep, the jet lag taking its toll.

The next day, they had an early breakfast and headed to the train to ride up to Kleine Scheidegg to ski. Angela's face was glued to the window as the alpine landscape passed by. At the summit, they disembarked and walked up a small ridge where they lined up with others, clicked on their skis, adjusted their goggles, and pushed off down the slope.

Angela was a good and aggressive skier but unsure of the terrain, so they remained close together, weaving between other skiers. They paused at the top of a steep drop off.

"Whoa! This looks daunting," Angela said.

"It would be in New England with ice, but the conditions here are different. Your edges will grip the snow easily. You'll see."

Bernard pushed off and made several carefully executed turns, and Angela followed. They skied up to another ridge where they stopped to look at the scenery.

"Wow, this is amazing!" Angela said excitedly.

"Just wait. You've only seen a fraction of what's available here."

They continued skiing down the trail to another lift. It was early, so they mounted the chair alone. It rose steeply through a field of fir trees covered in fresh snow. A man under the lift rode through fresh power, weaving between the gnarly trunks of the trees and shouting excitedly at the conditions.

Angela smiled.

She looked to the right at the impressive valley that included the village of Grindelwald, surrounded by towering peaks, forests, and expansive snow fields. To the left, a ridge rose above the runs with meters of snow resting on rocky terraces. She leaned into her father and kissed him on the cheek.

"I'm glad you like it," Bernard said. "I think I could live here."

"You're not thinking of moving, are you?" she said in alarm.

"No, it's just a fantasy. But a nice one!"

Angela looked relieved. They reached the top of the lift and skied off, resting at a large space where skiers were adjusting boots and goggles, ready for their runs.

Bernard leaned his face back and let the sun warm it.

"Ready to go?" she asked.

"Ready."

"Which direction?"

"Let's go this way. There are some pleasant runs and other lifts. There are also some nice on-mountain restaurants where we can stop for lunch later."

Angela nodded and followed her father as he began the descent.

They continued skiing, had a pleasant lunch, and then headed to town as Angela's jet lag kicked in. She took a nap on the sofa, and Bernard caught up on emails and reading in the bedroom.

A text came in, "Hey there. You still up for skiing tomorrow? We're looking forward to meeting your daughter." A photo of Theo popped up on the screen. It was a summer picture of him hiking, skin slightly red from the sun, hair tousled in the wind, and legs bulging out of his shorts.

"That would be great. 9 AM at the summit of the First gondola?"

"Perfect."

Bernard felt a little flutter in his stomach, not sure if it was nervousness or excitement or maybe both.

The next day they took the gondola up to the First mountain and grabbed a hot chocolate at the bar waiting for the Deckers. They sat in front of a panoramic window watching the sun rise higher over the tallest peaks, burning off the morning mist that clung to the steep mountainsides. A soft mellow light glowed through wispy clouds, drifting over a ridge in the distance. Snow on the rocky cliff below them clung tenaciously to patches of moss anchored on a wall of crumbly dark shale.

Zoe ran up from behind Bernard and grabbed his knees. Bernard turned and said, "Hey, Zoe! How are you doing? This is my daughter, Angela. Angela, this is the ski champion, Zoe!"

"Nice to meet you." Zoe stated in slow but confident English.

"The pleasure is all mine." Angela replied. "What a lovely ski jacket you have."

"It's new. My other one is *kaput*."

"Well, I like it. It's a nice shade of pink."

Zoe grinned. Theo and Jules strolled into the room, giving Bernard warm kisses on the cheek and greeting Angela.

"You didn't tell us how stunning your daughter is," Jules added. "I see the resemblance to her father's good looks."

"Ah, Jules, ever the diplomat."

Theo and Bernard stared at each other – an unspoken warning not to venture into recently unveiled secrets.

"Are we all ready to ski?"

"Absolutely," Theo stated enthusiastically.

The five of them headed up Oberjoch and made tracks on a light base of fresh powder. This was the first time Bernard had skied with the Deckers. Zoe was intrepid, trying to keep up with Angela with whom she developed a quick affinity. Jules was graceful – something Bernard had imagined. She was all about *belle forme* and appearance.

Theo skied aggressively, leaning down the mountain and making quick, sharp turns. He was faster than the rest and would stop, glancing uphill at everyone as they caught up. He fixed his attention on Bernard, who skiing just slightly ahead of the rest, came up to Theo and made a quick skid stop, throwing fresh powder onto Theo.

"*Scheisse!*

Bernard grinned, glancing uphill at his daughter, Zoe, and Jules.

Theo mumbled quietly, "So, you think you're quite the skier, huh? Just wait."

Everyone stopped for a moment, and then Theo skied off. Bernard quickly followed, skiing straight downhill, sparing no effort to catch up and pass him. He made a few showy turns and quickly slid to a stop.

"Okay, you showed me you can keep up. See that ridge over there? Let's see if you can handle what's just below it?"

They pushed off and arrived at the edge. Below was an extremely steep but thankfully short hill where fresh snow barely concealed tracks from previous days. This was Bernard's greatest nightmare, skiing off the groomed run through an unpredictable field of frozen crud and heavy snow. He glanced frighteningly down the slope and then in terror at Theo. He knew it was a bad idea to even consider the run, but also wondered if pushing beyond his comfort zone might not actually be a good thing – and he certainly didn't want to seem like a sissy. He looked back and forth at the slope and then at Theo. Theo gave him a daring stare.

Suddenly, Bernard leaned over the ridge and pushed off with his poles. He made one carefully planted turn, and then another, keeping his skis pointed downhill, minimizing the risk of snagging a pile of crusty snow under the surface. He made another series of turns and then glided onto the groomed trail below where Zoe, Angela, and Jules were anxiously hoping no one would get hurt. They applauded.

Theo followed, making the first two turns well, but snagged a ski on the third turn and went flipping into the air. He landed with a thud in a pile of soft snow at the edge of the groomed trail. His pride wounded, he pulled himself out of the drift, dusted the snow off his jacket, and skied over to his family.

"Well, it looks like our American is more of a skier than I thought," he conceded.

"Beginner's luck," Bernard retorted.

"Dad, I've never seen you ski like that before. When did you learn to do that?"

He wanted to respond that it was nothing compared with being cast adrift from work and family, but he decided he didn't want to laden her with his resentment. "I've been practicing," he said instead.

Theo put his arm around Jules's shoulder and whispered something in her ear. She smiled and then said, "Let's head up the Shilt lift. I want to show Angela my favorite run."

They continued down the mountain and skied up to the line at the bottom of the lift. They filed into place and then mounted the chair. Zoe was in the center, Theo and Bernard on the left, and Jules and Angela on the right. Jules leaned over affectionately toward Angela and inquired, "So, what do you think?"

"It's beautiful! I never imagined something so extensive and breathtaking."

"I mean, your dad."

"What do I think about my dad?" she asked curiously.

"Yes, how do you think he's doing?"

"So, you heard?"

"Yes, we did. Sounds like it was unexpected."

"In a way, yes. But I wasn't entirely surprised."

"What do you mean?"

"I don't know – sometimes you just have a feeling, an intuition about things."

"Hmm." Jules responded.

"He seems to have adjusted well to his situation here. And I'm grateful he has made some friends."

"It was a pleasant surprise for us, too, although the occasion was frightful."

"I heard. Glad Zoe is okay." She smiled over at Zoe, who was tapping her poles on her skis, taking in everything the adults were saying.

Bernard confessed to Theo that he was horrified at the idea of skiing down the steep hill and that it was only sheer luck that kept him from a tumble. Secretly, he was delighted that he had succeeded and hoped Theo thought of him as an equal. Theo's size and strength were enviable, and in comparison, Bernard felt himself middle-aged, out of shape, and in decline. It was just one short steep slope, but it jolted Bernard into recognition that he had the hutzpah to embrace new challenges and push himself.

They arrived at the top of Shilt and took an easy run to the right. The run sloped gently between two massive peaks, making a few thrilling undulations here and there. Farther down the run, the trail opened wide as it steepened. They gained speed, gliding between the high rising rocky walls and out onto a broad snow field that lay in front of the imposing Wetterhorn and Schreckhorn peaks, both covered in fresh snow. Angela looked over toward Jules who nodded, saying, "Isn't this beautiful?" Angela nodded back, grinning at the idyllic Alpine landscape before her.

They all stopped just above a series of runs down to another lift, quietly taking in the scenery. Fresh snow at the edge of the run glistened in the sunshine, mottled by blue shadows cast from a clump of majestic fir trees. Angela stood next to Zoe and Jules, who had quickly adopted her as their ski mate. Theo and Bernard stood nearby, clearly bonding as they skied together.

"Shall we have lunch soon – perhaps at Bort?" Theo inquired of the gang.

"I already made reservations, dear," Jules noted.

"Of course you did," Theo said playfully.

They skied to the next lift and then took another lift higher up before taking a series of challenging runs to the guesthouse and restaurant. They kicked off their skis and leaned them against the ski rack at the edge of the terrace. The maître d' showed them their table, set overlooking the valley below.

Angela couldn't contain herself, looking out over the scenery. She squeezed her dad tightly. "Thank you – this is incredible."

"I knew you would like it."

The terrace filled up quickly as the sun warmed the winter air. A family with a couple of older teens waved from across the deck.

Jules said to Theo as she waved back, "There's Werner and Margrit with their two sons, Marc and Felippe."

Bernard glanced over and recognized Marc from the gondola the other day. Felippe was older, perhaps college age. "You know them?" he mumbled to Theo.

"Yes, they are friends from our complex in town. Werner is an insurance executive, and Margrit is a philanthropist. Their sons are quite nice. I think Felippe is doing an internship with one of the NGOs in Bern. Here, let's introduce you."

Theo rose with Bernard and Angela while Jules remained with Zoe. "Werner, Margrit, good to see you on such a beautiful day. These are some new friends of ours from America – Bernard and his daughter Angela."

"Welcome," they said in perfect English. "These are our sons, Marc and Felippe."

They both rose, shook Theo's hand, and reached for Angela's hand. She reached out, first to Marc, the younger, and then to Felippe, the older. "It's nice to meet you," she said in perfect German.

Theo looked at Bernard inquisitively. Angela then added in German, "Beautiful day, no?"

The boys nodded, Felippe clearly drawn to Angela. She had taken her ski helmet off, and her wavy blond hair bounced playfully off the shoulders of her colorful ski coat. She placed her hand affectionately on Bernard's shoulder, turning up the charm. Theo, Bernard, and Angela returned to their table, Angela glancing back at Felippe.

"Nice family," Theo added at their table. "Jules, did you notice how grown up Felippe is becoming?"

"Yes, quite!" She glanced first at Bernard, then at Angela.

The server brought them their drinks and appetizers. "So, Angela, are you in school now or working?" Jules inquired.

"I'm in my first year of college."

"Where and what are you studying?"

"I'm at Brown, studying international economics."

"Hmm," Theo intoned. "I hear that's a great school."

"It's nice, although I'm not crazy about Providence. But it's good to get out of Boston."

"What do you want to do with your degree?" Jules inquired further.

"I'm not sure yet. Work for some international company."

"Your German is good. Do you speak other languages like your father?"

"Thanks. I work at it. I don't think I'm as good as dad, but I do speak French and Spanish besides German. I've taken some Mandarin, too."

"All good credentials for your career."

Angela smiled and took a long sip of white wine. She glanced over at Felippe, and Jules noticed.

"Bernard, are you and Angela free later this afternoon? Maybe we can meet up with Werner, Margrit, and their boys at a bar for a drink."

Angela's face lit up as she looked at her father.

"That would be nice if Angela is up for it."

"Why not? Isn't that what you do here?" she pressed.

"What about jet lag?"

"Dad, I'm fine – besides, it's a great way to practice German."

"Is that what it is?" Bernard inquired sarcastically.

A young woman came to the table and took their order. Angela ordered a salad, Bernard a schnitzel with *frites*, and Jules and Theo ordered the stew special. Zoe asked for a hamburger, showing off to her new American friend. A couple of crisp bottles of white wine were brought to the table, and they all raised a glass to a perfect day of skiing.

Bernard was glad to be establishing fresh memories at Bort, supplanting the ones he had formed with Susan a few years before.

He smiled fondly at Angela as she sipped her wine and picked at the salad. Zoe kept her attention focused on Angela and Bernard, rocking her legs gleefully under the table.

Jules and Theo leaned into each other as they enjoyed the stew. Bernard thought how perfect they were with each other – as if best friends. Jules's brunette hair shimmered in the light, and her caramel complexion seemed unusually luminescent. She smiled warmly at Bernard and nodded to him as she glanced at Angela, looking over at Felippe.

"Zoe, you're quite the skier," Angela began, engaging her new friend, who seemed isolated from all the adult conversations and exchanges.

"I took lessons last year," Zoe said proudly.

"My daddy gave me lessons when I was a girl, too. But it was much colder, and I was miserable," she said as she looked over at her dad.

"I remember those days fondly," Bernard noted, reaching his arm around his daughter.

"Have you ever raced?" Angela asked Zoe.

"No, but next year I can join the school ski team."

"That sounds great," Angela said warmly to Zoe, who was beaming with excitement.

"Bernard, where did you learn to ski so well?" Jules inquired.

"Over the years, I picked it up. My father's idea of ski lessons was taking us to the top of the lift and pushing us onto the icy run. We eventually learned how to stop before we hit the netting at the bottom of the hill."

Theo laughed. "I've hit a few of those in my day," he said, chuckling.

Jules hit Theo on the top of his hand and then looked up. "Don't fool yourselves! Theo's dad was a ski instructor. Theo was racing the Lauberhorn at the age of three."

Theo blushed. He lowered his head, poking at the stew in embarrassment, his tousled dirty blonde hair fluttering in the gentle breeze now blowing across the terrace. Bernard looked over at him, regarding his childlike affability.

They continued to visit, finished lunch, and took the gondola up to the top of the mountain, where they took the long five-mile run back to town. The trail was gentle and meandered between barns, summer huts, and ski chalets. From time to time, they would pause for a breather, take in the scenery, and then push off to continue their descent.

At the bottom of the mountain, they took off their skis and walked a few blocks to an outdoor bar where Werner, Margrit, Marc, and Felippe were already seated, drinking beer. They made room for Jules, Theo, Zoe, Bernard, and Angela – with Angela conveniently seated near Felippe and Marc. Marc continued to text his friends, and Felippe began in heavily accented English, "How was your skiing today?"

Angela replied enthusiastically in English, "It was magnificent. I've never seen a place as nice as this. You are so fortunate."

"Yes, we are. But you must have good skiing in New England, no?"

"It's okay, but nothing like this."

Some friends of Felippe walked up from across the street and, in French, said hello to him. He bantered back and forth with them and then introduced Angela.

"*Enchantée*," she said warmly in French.

Felippe looked over at Angela. "You speak French, too?"

"*Oui, bien sûr.*" She replied.

Felippe's friends visited for a while, hugged him goodbye, and shook Angela's hand. Felippe then leaned toward Angela and asked questions about what she was studying and what she was planning to do during her vacation in Grindelwald. Angela found Felippe very attractive. He was of similar build to his father — tall, lean, and athletic. He was graceful in his gestures and had a warm, broad smile.

Bernard glanced toward her, conveying his fatherly concern. She nodded as if to say everything was fine.

Theo leaned affectionately against Bernard and inquired, "Angela seems happy?"

"Yes, I haven't seen her like this in a while. She seems quite content. Thanks for introducing her to Felippe and Marc. It's nice for her to meet people her age."

"Felippe is a great kid with a wonderful future. Sounds like your daughter has a lot going for her, too."

"Yes, I just hope this divorce and my change in work status haven't dampened her plans."

"Kids her age are resilient, and she seems very confident and self-assured – in a good way."

"Yes, she gets that from her mother."

"From what I saw today, her father isn't a wimp. Isn't that what you say in English?" Theo stated emphatically, staring wide-eyed at Bernard, his face bathed in the warm sunlight.

"Did you think I was a wimp before today?" Bernard playfully inquired.

"Not at all, but I underestimated your willingness to push yourself."

"What was I to do? My daughter, Zoe, and Jules were all looking at me. I couldn't chicken out."

"I was hoping you might. I didn't want to ski it. It was full of frozen crud – perfect for a flip like I made."

"So, you're not as daring as you seem?"

"Well, I don't know if I would say that," he noted with a gleam in his eye.

Jules glanced over at Theo and Bernard and noted their playful exchange, like two schoolboys bragging about exploits. She reached for a few fries and put them in her mouth, continuing to observe their camaraderie. Bernard caught her eye, smiled, and pulled back away from Theo, realizing that perhaps he was too close and chummy for her comfort. He then addressed Zoe, "You were quite the skier today. I didn't know you were so brave!"

Zoe grinned and then handed Angela some fries. "Why thank you, Zoe. How did you know these are my favorite?"

Zoe took a sip of her hot chocolate and looked up at her mother, who asked. "Are you ready to head home?"

Zoe nodded no, but Jules was clearly ready to go, change clothes, and prepare dinner. She stood, put on her coat, and looked at Theo. He then turned to Bernard. "Looks like we are heading home. Would you like to meet up tomorrow to ski?"

Bernard looked at Angela, who then looked at Felippe. Felippe said, "We're going to be skiing at Kleine Scheidegg tomorrow. Do you want to meet up?"

Theo added, "We were going over there tomorrow, too. Should we meet someplace?"

Werner suggested a rendezvous place and time, and everyone paid their tab and bundled up for their walk home. Angela gave Felippe a kiss on the cheeks, and he embraced her warmly. Everyone else exchanged kisses and hugs and went their separate ways.

Angela and Bernard walked home. He placed his hand on her shoulder, and she looked up at him with a warm smile.

"Are you up for some pasta tonight? I have the makings for a few things, and we have salad and bread."

"Sounds perfect. I think I'll probably crash soon. It's been a long day."

"I hope you had fun. You seemed to get along nicely with Felippe."

Angela blushed. "He's nice."

"Any chemistry?"

"Dad!!!"

"Okay, I won't meddle. Just be careful."

She glared at him.

As they prepared dinner, Angela pressed her father with a question. "Any results from the dating app you were using in Boston?"

"Not lately. I haven't been signing in much."

"You have to do so regularly, or you will miss good opportunities."

"I'm not in a hurry."

"But you have to move on."

"I have. What do you think I'm doing here?"

"Having a good time, but you're not meeting people."

"I've met Jules and Theo – and now some of their friends."

"They're all couples. You need to meet singles, people who are available."

"I will."

They sat down for dinner and continued their conversation with Bernard, asking, "And you, have you met anyone at school yet?"

"There are a lot of nice guys, but they're pretty intellectual."

"You're at Brown. What did you expect?"

"I don't know. I thought it would be a little different. I keep meeting guys who are very nice, friendly, handsome – and gay."

"Hmm," Bernard sighed.

"There was this one guy. He seemed so outgoing and attentive. It was so easy to talk with him, and he seemed genuinely interested in me."

"But?"

"But he was gay."

"How did you know? Did he say something?"

"No, it was a few things. He always complimented me on what I was wearing and kept adjusting my scarf, coat, and other things. Then one day we were at a café, and I noticed him staring at a gorgeous guy across the room. We were talking, but he never looked me in the eye. I decided then I was done. It's too bad, he was really handsome. I still don't get it – guys who like guys."

"Yes, that can be confusing."

"It would be like you coming out suddenly. You're handsome, in good shape, and you like to ski – not particularly a sissy sport."

Bernard looked at her with consternation.

"Sorry, I guess that's a stereotype," she added.

"But how do you know?" Bernard inquired.

"You're asking me? How do I know if someone is gay? I guess you have to ask what they're attracted to. Like you were attracted to mom."

"But isn't sexuality more fluid, less of a binary thing?"

"That's what scholars say, but I haven't met very many people like that. Most people are attracted to one gender or the other," she noted.

"But there are more than two genders – at least that's what scientists say. And gender identity is complex – with many ways to be a man, to be a woman," Bernard elaborated.

"When did you get so interested in this topic?" Angela pressed her father.

"I don't know. I guess you get to a certain point in your life, and you begin to ask questions."

"About your own identity?"

"No, no," Bernard interjected quickly, "It's more philosophical - reflections on people you meet. You begin to appreciate how unique people are."

Angela poked at her food and took a sip of wine. She was ready to end the conversation, reaching for her phone and pressing to see if any new texts had come in.

"Do you mind if I go to bed soon? It's going to be a busy ski day tomorrow."

"Not at all. I'll take care of the dishes while you use the bathroom."

"Thanks, dad." Angela kissed Bernard and grabbed some things, going down the hall to the bathroom. Bernard opened the sofa bed for her, brought in a pillow and blankets, and then went back into the bedroom. He sat in the chair and looked out the window into the dark night, where the faint silhouette of the mountains loomed in the near distance.

He smiled as he considered all they had done during the day, and the good time he had with Theo and Jules. He was happy his daughter was with him, had met some friends, and was enjoying herself. The time in Switzerland was everything he had hoped it would be — a reset for his life and a respite from all the painful disruptions he had experienced during the last year.

He went into the bathroom after Angela finished, got ready for bed, and then slipped in under the fluffy duvet and fell into a sound sleep.

6

Chapter Six

The next morning, Bernard and Angela walked to the station to catch the train for Kleine Scheidegg. It was cloudy and seemed like it might snow at any moment. Bernard expressed concern about the conditions.

"Don't worry dad, I've skied when it was snowing before. It will be fine."

"I know, but I assure you, it is different here. We will be above the tree line, and visibility can become near zero. It's not fun."

"The webcam shows only partly cloudy skies up there. See?" She pointed to her phone.

Bernard nodded and continued to walk to the platform. They lined up with other skiers jockeying for space and ready to leap aboard the cars when the doors opened. Angela and Bernard stood at the edge of the platform and quickly entered the train car when it arrived, placing their skis in the rack and grabbing two seats near a large window. The train soon pulled out of the station, stopped briefly at the Grund station, and then continued its ascent up the mountain.

The train traveled through a burrow of iridescent blue as snow drifts reached high above the top of the carriage on the mountain side of the track. On the downhill side, the slate tile roofs of rustic wooden huts were laden with thick drifts of snow. Tracks left by wild goats, wolves, and hikers meandered between tall pines where the boughs arched under frozen deposits left in the overnight storm. Angela's face was glued to the window in amazement.

Bernard reviewed some texts from Theo, stating they had already arrived at the station. Conditions were not as poor as one imagined on the way up, but not as sunny as the day before. A photo of Theo popped up with the first text, and Bernard took a protracted look. He glanced over at Angela, hoping she hadn't noticed.

Once at the station, they quickly grabbed their skis and found the Deckers waiting near the tracks.

"Good morning, Angela," Jules said warmly, greeting her with kisses on her cheeks. "And Bernard – hmm." She pronounced his name with a strong French accent and kissed him warmly as well.

Bernard and Theo shook hands firmly, and Bernard reached down to give Zoe a hug. "You ready for a fun day of skiing?"

She nodded.

Everyone was bundled up for the cold. People stretched and warmed up on the sunny, flat terrain. Angela checked several pockets on her new coat, making sure she had lip balm, sunscreen, and her phone – and then looked up at the mountain as if she were ready to begin the day.

"Everyone set?" Theo inquired. "I thought we could ski this area for a while, then head over to Männlichen. Then perhaps we can make our way back to this side and hit Allmend for lunch."

Angela concealed a little smile as a text came in from Felippe, suggesting lunch at Allmend. 'What a coincidence,' she thought to herself.

They all pushed off the crowded gathering place and made quick sharp turns to avoid others. Once out of the crowd, their turns became relaxed, taking advantage of the soft, fresh snow. Visibility was good enough. They skied to the Honegg lift and then over to Tschuggen – where Bernard had run into Zoe after her accident. They stopped along the route.

"Zoe, here's where you started a fight with that tree," Bernard began.

"I think it won," she replied.

"Only temporarily. In the end, you beat it. See over there? It looks a little tattered," Bernard pointed.

Everyone chuckled. But Jules looked concerned, as if she finally grasped how close she came to losing her daughter to a more tragic accident.

"Shall we continue?" Theo proposed, adjusting his goggles and pushing off onto the trail.

They rode the Tschuggen lift to the top and began skiing down the varied terrain of Männlichen. Angela leaned over to her father at the top of the area. "This looks like another whole ski resort, and it's really just a section of the area. Amazing!"

"Yes, and if you ski to town, it's equivalent to two-and-a-half Vermont resorts stacked on top of each other."

Angela looked out over the horizon in amazement. They made their way down several trails that looked deceptively easy and boring from above, but were more interesting in reality – with trails narrowing into mogul fields and banks of snow forming natural half pipes ready for jumps and banked turns. Angela skied well, Bernard following closely and attentively behind her. Jules and Zoe stayed close together, leaving Theo to weave between Angela and Bernard.

On the rides up the lift, Bernard positioned himself next to

Theo, who always welcomed him with a warm, affable smile and an eagerness to chat and recount anecdotes of the last run. He felt a twinge of guilt not paying as much attention to Angela, although she seemed happy meeting new people and practicing languages. They eventually made their way over to the Wengen side of the mountain and to the Allmend restaurant for lunch. After propping their skis on the rack and going to the bathrooms, they found a table inside. Felippe and some friends wandered in shortly thereafter. He approached Theo and Jules, embraced them, shook Bernard's hand, and began speaking to Angela.

"I was hoping we might run into you!" he began.

Angela blushed slightly, looked guiltily over at her father, and then turned back to Felippe, who asked Angela, "Do you want to join us?"

She glanced inquisitively at her father, who nodded for her to join them. She grabbed her ski helmet and gloves and joined Felippe and his friends at another table.

Jules noted, "I think she's made a friend."

"I hope that's all," Bernard added.

"Do you want to sit where you can keep your eyes on her, or would you like to sit next to me?" Jules nudged him playfully.

"Why would I want to give up sitting next to you?"

"I thought that would be your answer," she leaned into him.

Zoe grinned as her mom and Bernard played. Theo grabbed Zoe's hand, and they opened the menu. "Are we going to get some *frites*?"

She nodded enthusiastically.

Bernard stood up and went to the bar to get a napkin as a pretext for walking toward Angela's and Felippe's table. She was laughing and clearly enjoying her new group of friends. He was cautiously proud of her.

Back at the table, he reviewed the menu and ordered a plate of bolognese and salad. Theo had already ordered wine. A few flakes of snow danced outside the large windows. It felt cozy to be inside and enjoy new friends.

Bernard sat opposite Theo and Zoe, next to Jules. Theo's knees grazed his, and he felt a charge of energy pass up his leg. Theo smiled and left his knees pressed against Bernard's. Bernard adjusted his leg, looking over at Theo, who, avoiding his gaze while stirring Zoe's hot chocolate, found his knees again and continued to press firmly. It was now obvious to Bernard that the gesture was intentional and unapologetic. He sought to conceal his embarrassment, nervously arranging utensils and spices on the table, and looking inquisitively at Jules, who was reviewing texts on her phone. He was relieved when the food arrived, thinking it would distract Theo and he could imperceptibly extract himself. For a moment, Theo's legs moved as he reached for his plate, but then, as he settled back into place, he pressed the side of his leg up against Bernard's, now more than just a knee awkwardly positioned. Bernard felt the warmth of Theo's long upper leg on his own. His initial response was alarm, a spontaneous reaction to male-male touch.

Jules glanced covetously at Bernard's plate, asking how the Bolognese tasted. He offered her some, which she took enthusiastically. "I just can't seem to make a good bolognese," she remarked.

"I can help with that. It's my grandmother's favorite dish."

"You're Italian?"

"Only a little, from one grandmother. We're still very English."

"Well, I knew there was something I liked about you," Jules added again, playfully.

As Jules flirted and Theo continued to press his leg, he thought of the time he and Susan and Alan were vying for attention more than twenty years ago. He wondered how ironic and strange that history repeats itself. Jules, the beautiful Susan – sensual, enchanting, seductive. Theo, the alluring Alan – mysterious, exotic, fiery.

Jules savored the bolognese. "Delicious," she said as she licked her lips of the sauce. She took a long sip of red wine to wash it down. She reached over again for another fork full, catching Bernard's eye as she twirled the spaghetti with her fork.

"Hey, don't I get some?" Theo shouted at Jules.

"Bernard, can Theo have some?" she asked with a certain playfulness.

Theo looked imploringly at Bernard, putting his hands together pleadingly.

"Well, I suppose so," as he pushed his plate toward Theo, who took a generous fork-full of pasta and sauce. In return, he offered Bernard some of his schnitzel. Bernard remarked to himself how uncharacteristic this sharing of food was for the Swiss and relished the familiarity he enjoyed with Theo and Jules, even if he was getting competing signals.

Theo was finishing his schnitzel, evading Bernard's increasingly inquisitive and alarmed looks. Jules detected Theo's change in mood and reached over to his plate to grab the last bite of veal.

"Hey, that was mine!" he declared.

"Oh yeah? It looks like it's mine now." She plopped it into her mouth.

Theo glared at her affectionately, then turned to Bernard, "And that is why she is so captivating – or should I say, that is why I am held captive."

Bernard laughed and then turned to look at Angela, who was enjoying her new friends. Out of the window, he noticed snow had begun to fall more steadily. "Well, do we continue skiing?" he inquired of Jules and Theo.

"I'm not sure I'm up for much more. Why don't we ski into town? We can take the train back to Grindelwald from there."

Zoe grinned and looked over at Angela. Bernard then asked Zoe, "Should we ask Angela to join us or let her go her own way with her friends?"

Zoe replied, "I think she should go with her friends."

"My thought exactly," Bernard replied with a wink.

Bernard walked over to Angela's table, met her new friends, and shook hands warmly with Felippe. Angela was delighted to have the opportunity to ski alone with them. "I can meet you later for dinner."

"If you have other options, that's fine with me as well. I don't mind a quiet evening at home."

She smiled and gave her dad a warm hug.

Jules, Zoe, Theo, and Bernard headed out, grabbed their skis, and then headed down the slope toward the village. The snow was falling lightly and made for one of those enchanting runs past barns, chalets, and brightly lit shops lining the run into Wengen. When they got to the center, the snow stopped, and peaks of blue sky appeared.

"Hey, you up for a run from Männlichen back to Grindelwald? We can take the cable car up and ski home. We'll be there faster than if we take the train," Theo explained.

"Why not?" Bernard replied. Jules and Zoe nodded affirmatively, and they lined up for the next cable car to arrive.

When the doors opened, the crowd of people waiting on the platform spilled in as if they were getting onto a subway in New York or London during rush hour. Bernard, Theo, Zoe, and Jules were part of the first wave and made their way to the wall of glass on the opposite side of the car. "At least we will have a view," Jules noted.

Theo's back was against the glass, and Bernard was in front of him. As the crowd pressed in, he was pushed up against Theo. Jules was nearby, blocking Zoe from the crowd with her skis. The doors shut, and the cable car lurched out of the station into the open air. Bernard was uncomfortably close to Theo and found it difficult to concentrate on anything but preserving what little distance between them he could. It was a losing battle with the weight of the crowd continuing to squeeze against him. He slid his skis in between them, but that wasn't enough to prevent Theo from leaning into Bernard, his legs searching for space between Bernard's legs.

Inches apart, Bernard scrutinized the creases around Theo's hazel eyes, the contours of his nose, the hint of stubble on his chin, and a few playful locks of blond hair that had spilled out from under his helmet onto his forehead. He felt himself becoming aroused and looked out of the window over Theo's shoulder, but the physical sensation didn't dissipate.

The cable car passed a pylon, and the car rocked. Bernard shifted his weight, and Theo reactively grabbed Bernard's shoulder to maintain his own balance. They stared at each other.

"Whoa," Theo interjected defensively. "I am still not used to these things swinging 500 meters above the ground."

"Me either," Bernard agreed, hoping to diffuse the awkward intimacy. Theo removed his hand from Bernard's shoulder, but kept his leg pressed into Bernard's. "You okay over there, Jules?" Bernard inquired.

"We're fine. You guys?"

"Fine," Theo said without elaboration, looking out of the window to avoid Bernard's eyes but keeping his leg pressed firmly against Bernard's.

The car arrived at the terminus, and they were the first to leave as the doors on their side of the car opened first. Bernard sighed deeply, taking in huge breaths of fresh, cool air. He watched Theo march up the ridge before him, the backs of his legs flexing with each step forward. He tossed his skis onto the snow, stepped into the bindings, and stood in a relaxed pose as he glanced back at Bernard, Jules, and Zoe following.

"Shall we ski all the way to town?" Jules asked.

"Absolutely," Bernard replied, eager to enjoy a nice long run.

He glanced over at Theo inquisitively, and Theo looked back as if nothing out of the ordinary had just transpired in the cable car.

The run was longer than Bernard remembered, traversing vast snow fields, weaving through thick forests, and snaking past barns and huts, some converted into make-shift bars. They paused from time to time, letting Zoe catch up and taking in the views of the village below.

When they arrived at Grindelwald Terminus, they took the shuttle bus to town. Jules suggested that she and Zoe return home to make dinner, giving Theo and Bernard time to get a drink alone.

Theo suggested a warm bar at a hotel on the main street where stone walls and a crackling fire created a pleasant space for people to gather and recount stories from their day on the slopes. Theo ordered a beer and Bernard some wine. They shared a small flatbread.

They sat facing each other awkwardly, waiting in silence for their drinks to arrive. Theo fussed with the menu, avoiding eye contact. Bernard stared at him intensely. "*Et alors*?" he asked discretely in French.

"*Et alors que*?" Theo responded, pretending ignorance as to the meaning of Bernard's inquiry – 'and so?'

The drinks arrived. Theo raised his glass to Bernard's, and each took a long sip. Theo looked back down pensively at his beer, tilting the glass from side to side.

"It was a nice day," Bernard began.

Theo nodded, continued to look at his glass, and said, "Um-hum." He then rubbed his forehead and looked up slightly, as if he were about to say something, but didn't.

Bernard looked increasingly worried, as if Theo were upset. Then he noticed a tear run down Theo's cheek and onto the napkin laying on the table. Surprised, Bernard implored. "*Dis-moi* – tell me."

"Stop with the French!" Theo reacted angrily, looking up and staring at Bernard. "English - no misunderstanding."

"What then?"

Theo looked intensely at Bernard, his eyes red. He said softly but deliberately, "I like you."

Bernard paused, surprised by the emotional declaration, and inquired, "What's the problem?"

Theo rubbed his eyes, took a sip of beer, and repeated, "I like you. It's not a problem, but it is a big deal."

Bernard began to realize the magnitude of what Theo was trying to express and replied, "I like you, too."

Theo smiled timidly, but with some skepticism, asked, "In the same way?"

"I think so," Bernard responded, realizing he was walking down a path he had never walked before. He believed he knew what Theo meant by his own declaration and realized he was, ever so timidly, admitting that he had similar feelings — physical and emotional feelings — for Theo.

It felt like a big step, a leap, a crossing – one without precedent or foundation. "Could this be happening?" he murmured almost imperceptibly to himself. He thought immediately of Susan and of Jules. He was attracted to them – to sensual lips, long necks plunging into firm breasts, and feminine charm – the aesthetic flare of women for color, fabric, intonation and, most of all, the way they could speak with their eyes. But he had definitely felt a connection with Theo, an undeniable fascination with this strong but emotional man sitting in front of him, and it felt oddly comforting.

"I hoped you might," Theo added, breaking Bernard's train of thought.

Bernard paused. "But, what about Jules?"

"Ah, Jules. Yes, that's a long story."

"But you love her, no?"

"Of course, I do. She's wonderful – my best friend."

"But I sense there is a 'but' to your statement." Bernard realized that as he pressed Theo, it was complicated. He knew all the theories about sexual orientation, that people were rarely 100% one way or the other. He had been attracted to Susan. Why wouldn't Theo be attracted to Jules? She was so beautiful.

Theo didn't respond. An awkward silence ensued. Theo got up and moved over to the small banquette on which Bernard was sitting, both now facing the room, loud and crowded with skiers meeting up after a long day on the slopes. No one paid them any attention. Theo slipped his hand under Bernard's thigh and reached for his beer with the other hand.

In a low voice, Bernard surprised himself and blurted out, "I knew the first night. You squatted in front of me to stir the logs in the fire. That was on purpose, wasn't it?"

"I don't know what you're talking about?" he said, grinning sheepishly. Then, seeking reassurance, he asked, "So, are you okay?"

"With what?"

"With what I just said and with my hand under your leg?"

"Well, it's all a little unexpected."

"I didn't expect it either."

"But you seem more comfortable with it," Bernard observed.

"Not entirely. And you?"

Bernard shook his head no. It struck Bernard that they were like adolescents making awkward first attempts at love – two chrono-logical adults who had skipped lessons long ago, following a script they had been handed but which no longer seemed to fit.

Bernard then asked, "Weren't you afraid to say what you said? Afraid of how I might respond?"

"Yes. You seemed enthralled with Jules. She's very seductive, and you seemed smitten."

"But you didn't seem too nervous to press my legs today – twice, I might add."

"Well, I was pretty sure you wouldn't object. Jules caught you," Theo said, now more animated.

"What?"

"It was the first night. When she sat next to me stroking my neck and looking over at you, she caught you. You were looking at me. She knew right away."

"But that's impossible."

"Jules is good. She's very observant. She knows."

"Does she know about you?"

"Yes."

"What does that mean?"

"It's a long story."

"I have time."

"When Jules first began her career, she entered a male-dominated industry. She wasn't married, and so the company asked her to travel a lot for work. Her colleagues were jealous of her success. She was smart, attractive, and good for business. One of her partners, and I'm now convinced he was uncertain of his own sexuality, tried to seduce her during a conference in the States. She rejected his overtures, and he persisted. He had connections, and he threatened to give her bad reviews if she didn't sleep with him. She reported it to human resources, who explained that it was difficult to prosecute such a case. She filed a complaint with a government commission, and the person hearing her case was a friend of mine."

"At that time, being openly gay in the Swiss government, particularly in international relations, wasn't a safe thing. No one would overtly discriminate, but one didn't advance if there were questions. So, I was discreet. My friend introduced us."

"I fell head over heels in love with Jules. In retrospect, I realize I was in love with her aesthetic sensibilities and sensuality. We were best friends. I loved shopping with her, picking out scarves that would go with sexy one-piece dresses she bought for cocktail parties we attended at her company. There was a campy playfulness between us – one we turned on in public to throw off her colleagues and, unconsciously, keep the closet doors closed on my account. It was easy to 'pass' as a straight man with Jules, and it continues to be."

"But what about sex?"

"I thought I could sustain the marriage and play my role. Jules was easy to love, and with enough porn, I could satisfy her."

"Did she suspect?"

"Eventually. I don't really know when it happened, but we eventually recognized it. We were still best friends and loved Zoe, so we stayed together for her sake – even for our sakes."

"But isn't that unfair to her – to you? You both deserve people you really connect with."

"We've discussed different options. We don't want an open marriage, and we don't want to divorce."

"What else does that leave you?"

"Until you showed up, we hadn't come up with anything."

"Ahh," Bernard sighed nervously. "Are you suggesting?" he stopped short of naming it.

"A throuple - I think you say in English?"

Bernard nodded.

"No, I don't think that's what we want."

"What do you want?"

"I think we're way ahead of ourselves here. I just said, 'I like you.'"

"Oh," Bernard responded dejectedly.

Theo pulled his hand out from under Bernard's thigh and placed his hands on Bernard's crotch under the table. "Don't look sad. I have a good feeling about you – Jules and I both do."

"But there you go again – Jules and I," Bernard protested.

Theo pulled his hand away from under the table, took a long sip of beer, and said, "Why don't we discuss more of this over dinner?"

"But what about the others?"

"Jules and Zoe are fine. Why don't you check with Angela? I'm sure she's happy to spend time with Felippe."

Theo requested the check, and Bernard texted Angela, who was quite delighted to have a free evening out with Felippe and his friends.

"I know a nice quiet restaurant in town – the back room of the Kreuz und Post. The front is busy, but on a night like this, there should be a quiet booth in the back. I know the chef, and he will take good care of us."

"Sounds good. Let's go."

They stood up, put on their coats, grabbed their gloves, and headed out into the night air. The walk from the bar to the hotel was short. The maître d' recognized Theo and accommodated his request for a quiet table.

"This is a nice place. I didn't know it was here," Bernard began.

"Most people just see the bar out front or think the restaurant is part of the hotel – which it is. But it is really a cozy and unique place known for some traditional family recipes that continue to be town favorites."

In the soft light of the restaurant, Theo's eyes were dark and mysterious. He rested his hand teasingly close to Bernard's, close enough for Bernard to feel its warmth. He wanted to reach over but held back out of respect for Swiss custom, although it would be anyone's guess they were on a date.

"Why me?" Bernard began.

"You came to Zoe's aid. She connected with you right away. Jules and I were both amazed. Zoe isn't normally friendly or playful and, with you, it was as if you were part of the family. Then, of course, I couldn't resist your eyes - warm and alluring. I love the dark hair that lies on your neck and the classy way you hold yourself – trim, elegant, thoughtful. I love your maturity – a maturity that hasn't dulled a youthful exuberance for life. Most of all, and you'll probably think this is strange, I had seen you in one of my dreams before – an English man, a skier who I almost bumped into on the slopes. We both apologized for the near mishap, stared at each other, and then skied on. It was you."

Bernard felt his stomach tighten. He was unfamiliar with the sensation of a man describing him romantically, affectionately. But he had noticed the same things - Theo's deep-set dreamy eyes, his strong muscular frame, broad shoulders, and a brooding mystique. Was he too afraid to admit it? What would it be like to let go, to let someone really love him, to have to learn a whole new language?

Bernard blushed. "*Et alors?*"

"What is it with you and French?"

"It's a sexy language."

"So, *alors*, you are sexy."

"Is that a question or a statement?"

"It could be both," Theo replied.

"A diplomat."

"Yes."

Theo wasn't entirely convinced Bernard was into him, even into men. "*Et alors, avec les hommes?*" It was easier to ask awkward questions in another language.

"Ah, *les hommes*," Bernard sighed.

"Yes, men. Do you like them?"

"Well, that's complicated."

"Usually is. Any experiences?"

"No," Bernard lied. The question brought up a troubling memory, one he had worked hard to repress over the years. As a 13-year-old, his uncle had molested him. He was an odd man – conservative, religious, and yet fun and playful. He showed up at family gatherings with his wife and kids, but rarely spent time visiting with the adults. He preferred playing football, soccer, or other sports with the young people. He seemed to have a lot of affection for Bernard, who, compared to his more athletic cousins, was less developed and a bit frail. Uncle Eddy, as they called him, would pull Bernard aside and ask him how he was doing, how was school, what new things he was learning. Bernard liked the attention and looked forward to Uncle Eddy's visits. One warm afternoon at the shore, when everyone else had gone to the house for lunch, Uncle Eddy remained on the beach with Bernard. They sat just where the waves were lapping on the beach, rushing over their tan bodies. Bernard noticed Uncle Eddy's crotch had grown erect. He felt a stirring in his own, and Uncle Eddy reached over. He had difficulty remembering what happened next. Several therapists had tried to help him recover the memory, but to no avail. He and Uncle Eddy never interacted again, and Bernard always worried for his younger cousins. Most importantly, whatever had happened, it kept him from feeling relaxed and in touch with his own sexual feelings – even for women. Theo's simple question – 'no experiences?' – triggered a recall that was frightening.

"What's the matter, Bernard?" Theo noticed Bernard's hand was trembling and his face had gone blanch. He reached over and Bernard quickly pulled his hand away.

"Sorry," Theo said, looking intently at Bernard, now irritable.

"It's my fault. I'm sorry. I overreacted."

"I apologize if I'm too forward."

"That's not it." Bernard hesitated, having never shared the story of Eddy with anyone other than his therapists. "I was molested." There, he said it. He got it out. He felt his body relax.

"Oh, I'm so sorry. Tell me about it." Theo was worried this was the wrong thing to ask, but Bernard was visibly relieved and seemed eager to get it off his chest.

Bernard recounted the story to Theo and acknowledged that the repressed memory screwed him up. He was always afraid to become like Eddy, and the thought of sex with a man triggered shame, fear, and pain. The idea of a relationship with a man wasn't off-putting. In fact, it was something he often thought of, but he couldn't get past the fear.

"We can take it slow – that is, if you want to pursue things."

Their entrées arrived. It gave Bernard a brief respite, a moment to process the quickly unfolding revelations. He looked up from his plate at Theo, attacking his *steak au poivre*. He had pulled up the sleeves of his pullover, exposing muscular forearms. Bernard liked his dark blonde hair, tousled after a day on the slopes. He fantasized about kissing his angular neck and caressing his broad shoulders. He felt himself becoming aroused. He lingered over his thoughts and, just as Theo looked up, he glanced evasively downward at his plate.

Theo stared at Bernard until he looked up, both smiling as if they had won some secret prize. Their gaze was filled with a quiet reassurance that they would be tender and thoughtful toward each other, both wounded, anxious.

Theo broke the silence, "*Et alors?*"

"Now you in French."

"What do we do?"

Bernard replied, "Finish dinner."

"What's for dessert?" Theo realized, just as he asked the question, that it was corny. But he was still too self-conscious to say what he wanted outright.

Bernard reached for his glass of wine and brushed Theo's hand. It amazed him how charged such a simple gesture could be. He took a long sip, the subtle flavors of the wine trickling down his throat. He hesitated a bit and then said, "Would you like to come over for a brandy – or something?"

Theo could hardly contain himself. He nodded.

They finished their dinners, skipped dessert, and headed to

Bernard's apartment. Theo texted Jules, who sent him an encouraging message back. Bernard's heart was racing. Fearful and excited, he reached for Theo's hand. They were both bundled up for winter, and Bernard rehearsed in his head how he might ceremoniously help Theo off with his ski clothes.

Their pace quickened as they climbed the stairs and opened the door to Bernard's apartment. It was quiet, dark, Angela still out with her friends. Before Bernard could turn on the light, Theo grabbed the back of Bernard's head and pulled him close, giving him a heated, moist kiss. He paused and said, "I've been waiting all night to do that."

Bernard kissed him back. He thought how interesting it was to be kissing a man at 50. It felt surprisingly natural, the rough stubble of Theo's beard reassuring, an odd reminder that he was with a man. He felt the solidity of Theo's body pressed against his. He pulled back slightly and began to unzip Theo's coat.

They stumbled into the living area. Bernard turned on a small table lamp, the yellow glow filling the room. They let their coats fall to the floor and embraced each other, both panting heavily. Bernard extracted himself nervously and inquired, "Shall I make a fire?"

"Sure, that would be nice." Theo wrung his hands as if looking for something to do.

"Can you pour us some drinks? There are glasses and brandy in the kitchen."

Bernard put some kindling in the fireplace and lit a match to ignite it. Warm yellow flames leaped up and singed the resin on the stacked logs. Theo came back with their drinks. He handed one to Bernard; they clinked the glasses, and each took a sip.

Part of Bernard wanted to rip Theo's clothes off and throw him to the ground, explore his body, consume him. But he held back, inviting him to sit on the sofa across from the fire. Theo, instead, was more eager to express himself, reaching first for Bernard's hand and looking for permission to do more. He moved closer and pressed himself firmly against Bernard. He put his arms around Bernard's shoulder.

Bernard leaned away but turned his head toward Theo with curiosity and desire. He began to speak, and Theo placed his finger on Bernard's lips, "Sh." He leaned more into Bernard, who fell back onto the sofa. His shirt sprung free of his pants, exposing a taut abdomen that Theo caressed, moving slowly up Bernard's chest. "Ahh, you feel so warm."

Bernard felt himself tremble and then relax. He leaned his head back, enjoying the movement of Theo's hands over his stomach. He reached down and pulled his shirt up over his head. Theo rose and removed his pullover and undershirt. In the soft orange light of the fire, Theo's powerful upper body came into focus – his broad muscular chest covered by a subtle light coat of dark blond hair. The tenderness and affection that was being expressed by this formidable masculine being in front of him made him want to cry. In all the years of making love to Susan, he never felt so validated as a man.

Theo reclined on Bernard, caressing the dark, soft hair on his chest. "I have always been fond of dark English men."

Bernard shook slightly, adrenaline rushing through his body. He felt anxious, troubling emotions flooding his unconscious. He fought to regain control and blurted out, "And I like muscular blondes."

"Have there been many?"

"Only one."

Bernard breathed in Theo's manly scent - earthy, sweet, subtle. He rose and opened his mouth for Theo's, both savoring the warmth of their lips pressed together. Bernard felt himself become increasingly aroused as Theo's hardness pressed against him. Bernard wanted to reach down and hold Theo, but he held back. Theo began to play with Bernard's belt and zipper, and Bernard became notice-ably anxious.

"Sorry, I don't mean to upset you," Theo said thoughtfully.

Bernard just nodded, rolling over to get out from under Theo. "I have to take it slow."

"I understand."

They both reached for their glasses of brandy, took a long sip, and just stared at each other. "You're so handsome," Theo began.

"Are you kidding? I'm a middle-aged man. You're - well, look at you – incredible!" Bernard exclaimed.

"Seriously, Bernard, you are very attractive. A thoughtful man wrapped up in a lean, taut body." He stroked his upper arm, "I love the hint of olive complexion in your skin," and then rubbing his eyes, "and the sparkle in these orbs."

Bernard rubbed his hands over Theo's thighs. "And you – a sexy Swiss farmer with a British accent – sophistication and raw mascu-line force!"

"Sounds like you've been giving this some thought."

"Well, your spell was having an effect."

Theo grinned. "*Et alors?*"

Bernard looked at his watch. "Angela will be home soon. Maybe we should call it a night. I'm sure Jules is wondering what's hap-pened as well."

Theo looked disappointed. "I hate to."

"Me, too. But let's not mess this up."

Theo nodded reluctantly. He stood up, grabbed his pullover, and put it on. Bernard put his own shirt on and tucked it into his pants. Theo pulled Bernard toward him. "Thanks for being so accepting." He pulled up Bernard's shirt and rubbed his hands over his chest.

"Thank you. What an unexpected gift," he said with a warm smile, looking into Theo's eyes.

Theo leaned over and gave Bernard another enthusiastic kiss, rubbed his back, and squeezed him tightly. Bernard rested his head on Theo's shoulder and then held his arms, putting a little distance between them.

"When will I see you again?"

"Maybe tomorrow?" Theo asked.

Bernard nodded. "I'll talk to Angela."

They kissed again. Bernard helped Theo on with his coat, opened the door, and let him out. He lingered with the door open until Theo had retreated out of sight down the stairs.

He closed the door. "Oh, my God!" he said to himself. "What the fuck?" He laughed. "You just kissed a man – you just played with a man's naked chest. What were you thinking?" He continued to talk to himself out loud. "Of all the crazy things," he continued blurting, not knowing where to go with his thoughts.

He plopped himself down on the sofa, breathing in Theo's lingering scent. He reached for his glass of brandy and took a long sip and said, "You wake up one day a straight man and go to bed gay. How does that happen? What am I going to say to Angela? Nothing. I'm not even sure if this is real or not. *Calmati* – calm down!" he admonished himself in Italian, trying to steady his nerves and excitement.

He heard Angela coming up the steps. He nervously looked around to see if anything was out of place. He noticed Theo's glass and quickly picked it up, ran to the kitchen, emptied it, and washed it, placing it back in the cupboard. Angela opened the door, unwrapped her scarf, and hung her coat on the hook just inside the door.

"Angela, back so soon?" he asked.

"It's not that early. We had dinner and drinks. It was fun." Angela walked into the center of the room and gave her father a hug.

"Do you want something to drink?" Bernard inquired.

"No, I'm good."

"I'll let you go to bed if you're tired."

"Yeah, I'll probably hit the sack soon. It was a fun day."

"Glad you liked it. It's so nice having you here," he added.

She smiled, got up, and went to the bathroom to get ready for bed. She came out with her pajamas. Bernard pulled out the sofa bed and brought in a pillow and blankets from the bedroom. "You have everything you need?"

"Yea, dad. Thanks. See you in the morning?"

"Yes. Goodnight."

"Goodnight," she replied.

Bernard went back into the bedroom and sat in the easy chair facing a large window. It was overcast and light snow was falling. He was now more composed, and he began to review the day's events. Everything felt surreal, a mirage. Had a muscular Swiss man really come onto him, and had he responded? Had he been comfortable with it? His body was tired, but his mind was racing. He pulled off his clothes and slipped in under the covers of the bed, resting under the puffy folds of the duvet and finding a soft spot for his head on the pillow. He closed his eyes. He tossed and turned for a while, but eventually fell to sleep.

7

Chapter Seven

The next morning, Bernard was in the kitchen making coffee, and Angela was asleep on the sofa bed. Bernard checked email, and a text came in from Theo.

"Good morning, handsome. Are you up for skiing? Jules and I decided to take the day off and stay in Grindelwald."

Bernard texted back, "That's great. Do you want to meet up someplace?"

"Kleine Scheidegg – at 10?"

"Perfect. I'll bring Angela."

He poured a cup of coffee for Angela and woke her. As she stirred, he stoked the embers in the fireplace and threw on a few logs.

"Did you have a nice time with Felippe and his friends?"

"We did. We went to a club. It was nice. He's nice."

"And?"

"And what?"

"Well, is there something more?"

"Dad, we just met."

"But you're good at vibes. What vibes are you picking up?"

"He's nice. I like him."

Angela went to the bathroom and, when she returned, went to the kitchen, where she poured some muesli into a bowl and spooned some yogurt onto it. "They have the best muesli here!"

"I know."

She went into the living room, sat down in front of the fire, and then picked up an undershirt off the side table. "I found this in between the cushions last night. It doesn't look like it's yours."

Bernard took it, embarrassed, and replied, "Maybe it belonged to the last tenant."

"I thought so, too, but I would have found it the first night."

"Hmm."

Angela scrutinized her dad.

"By the way, the Deckers are staying in town for another day. Would you like to ski with them – or do you have plans with Felippe?"

"He's going back to Bern. I'd love to ski with them. They're fun."

"I told them we'd meet them at Kleine Scheidegg at 10. Is that good?"

Angela nodded. She began checking texts and emails and then went into the bathroom to get ready. Bernard looked at Theo's undershirt in his hands and contemplated what to do with it and whether Angela had suspected anything. He tucked it under some of his things in a drawer in the bedroom. He pulled on his own thermal underwear, ski pants, and pullover - ready for a day of skiing.

Angela came out of the bathroom in a tight-fitting sweater, stretch ski pants, and suspenders. She was drying her hair in front of the fire when Bernard came into the room. She looked out the window. "It looks like a great day. Will it be too warm for this?"

"Bring layers. You can always adjust."

"By the way, dad, I like the ski outfit you have. Where did you get that? Looks like something mom would have picked out for you."

Wounded by the insinuation of his lack of taste, he replied, "If you have to know, I picked them out myself when I first got here. So, you like them?"

"Yes. The colors go well with your complexion, and the cut looks good on you."

"Thanks, dear."

"Are you okay?" she inquired. "I mean, with mom leaving and all."

"It was hard at first, as you know. But I'm adjusting. Being here has been good."

"Don't you feel alone here? Two months is a long time to be away from Boston."

"If it gets bad, I'll come home early," Bernard promised, thoughts of the evening with Theo assuring him it would be unnecessary. He wondered if two months was going to be long enough, if he might not end up remaining longer, exploring a new chapter in his life.

"What are you going to do next — I mean, in terms of work?"

"I don't know yet, but I have some ideas."

Angela looked relieved.

They pulled on their ski boots and gathered gloves, helmet, googles, and other accessories – and their skis – and headed out the door for the station. Once at Kleine Scheidegg, they quickly found the Deckers and took the Lauberhorn lift to the top of the mountain. It was a crystal-clear blue-sky day with freshly groomed conditions and no wind. Angela took off first, followed by Zoe and Jules. Bernard and Theo took up the rear. They wound their way along the ridge and over to the Wixi lift, where they took a nice broad run to the base area. Zoe enjoyed weaving around Angela. Jules was content making smooth graceful turns on her own, undoubtedly deep in thought. Theo made quick forceful turns, easily surpassing everyone and then stopping to wait for them.

Bernard wrestled with the urge to be more solitary, processing all that had occurred the night before with a competing desire to play. He skidded up to Theo, tossing fresh powder on him. Theo, in turn, took off quickly, daring Bernard to follow. Bernard did, and Theo let him catch up but, when he did, he gave him a bit of a nudge causing Bernard to almost catch an edge and fall. They stared at each other. Theo raced off. Bernard pursued him.

At the lift, Bernard lined up with Angela and Zoe while Jules and Theo ended up with a couple of teens. "You are skiing more aggressively than usual, dad. What happened to you?"

"I don't know."

Zoe tapped her skis with her poles, looking over at Angela and Bernard. She smiled warmly at Bernard. Bernard sensed she had some inkling about things unfolding.

They dismounted at the top, and Bernard skied close to Zoe and Angela. Zoe was an intrepid skier. Angela had a playful teenage style to her, taking advantage of the forgiving conditions. She clung to the side of the trail, kicking up some fresh ungroomed powder. They had gotten ahead of Theo and Jules. Bernard stopped on the side of the trail and waited for them to catch up. They looked like such a happy couple. He wondered what Theo had told Jules, and how Jules might be taking the news that her husband was in love.

They skied up to him, this time Jules skidding close to Bernard and playfully tossing snow onto him. It was a sign that she either didn't know what was going on or was fine with it. "Shall we ski over to the Eigernordwand lift?" Jules asked.

Bernard and Theo nodded. Angela and Zoe were busy taking selfies with the Eiger in the background. As the adults pushed off, they followed. On the next lift, Jules nudged her way next to Bernard and faked a fumble of her gloves. Theo, Angela, and Zoe caught a chair, Bernard and Jules followed on the next.

She began, "*Et alors?*"

"So, you know?" Bernard asked nervously.

She nodded. "Yes, Theo told me – at least all that was suitable to share."

Bernard blushed. He wasn't sure what to say.

She continued, "I know it may seem strange, but I'm happy for you."

"But it seems unfair to you."

"Believe it or not, I'm relieved."

"How is that possible?"

"Don't get me wrong, I love Theo. He's a wonderful friend, and I've always found him very attractive."

"But?"

"I don't know if Theo told you or not, but I was sexually harassed at work. He doesn't know the full extent of it. It was pretty terrible - with some rather frightening encounters with one of my former co-workers. Long story short, sex has become increasingly traumatic for me."

"Wow, I'm so sorry."

"I've worked a lot to get through it, but I just can't seem to shake it."

"So, what does Theo know?"

"He only knows that a colleague made advances. At some level, he thinks our sexual issues are his fault and, in part, they are. I know this isn't very noble of me, but it is convenient to have him feel responsible. I can leverage a lot of things from that."

"Quite the devil, then?" Bernard commented, not entirely surprised.

"I can use my feminine charms when I need to."

"I imagine you can."

"I thought I could work you, but look what happened?"

"Something tells me you aren't through with me yet."

She smiled. The chair arrived at the top of the lift, and they skied off. Theo and the others were waiting in the sun, ready to take the run down. "Shall we go for lunch soon? Wengen or just down there at the bottom of the run?"

Bernard chimed in, "I vote for Wengen – or rather, Allmend, on the way to Wengen."

Theo smiled. It was quickly becoming their place.

They took a steep expert trail from the top of Eigernordwand. The snow was soft but, on the steep part, there was a slick under-surface. Theo made a turn and caught ice, sliding out of control for a few yards. He finally caught some snow and skidded to a stop. His heart raced, and he felt unnerved. The others veered away from where he slid and circled around him. He adjusted his boots and jacket, took a couple of deep breaths, and regained composure.

They all pushed off and made their way along an easier trail that meandered through a beautiful forest of pines laden with fresh snow. The towering trees formed a corridor that was almost medita-tive, an easy path where one could relax and just enjoy being in the mountains. Zoe took the lead through the forest. The forest opened to a broad field where the Allmend restaurant overlooked the valley below. Zoe skied up to the rack outside the restaurant, kicked off her skis, and walked confidently toward the restaurant terrace. The maître d' welcomed her, and she asked in her most grownup voice, "We'd like a table for five."

"This way, *mademoiselle*." Zoe followed and began to organize seats at the table.

When the adults arrived, Zoe invited Angela and Jules to sit next to her. "The men can sit there. We'll sit here." Zoe seemed proud of herself, directing the adults.

Bernard and Theo had seats facing the town of Mürren across the deep ravine below them. Up on the mountain top was the famous Shilthorn Piz Gloria station where the James Bond film took place. A few paragliders were floating over the dramatic glacier-formed valley. They ordered drinks and meals. Angela stirred Zoe's hot choc-olate for her and, as she did so, looked over at her dad. He seemed engrossed in Theo, and it was at that moment she realized what was happening. Theo had unbuttoned his pullover in the warm sun, and Angela recognized the same color and brand undershirt she found on the sofa. She was stunned, even disgusted. It had never occurred to her that her father might be gay. Then she wondered if it was just a phase, a reaction to her mom's leaving him. She scrutinized them more carefully, searching for clues.

Jules noticed Angela's creased forehead and jumped in quickly, her territorial instincts kicking in. "Angela, you mentioned the other day that you are studying international finance at Brown. That's quite impressive."

"Oh, yes," she replied to Jules without elaboration, still scruti-nizing Theo and Bernard.

"What are your plans after graduation?"

Angela was annoyed with the questions. She wanted to interro-gate her dad instead. She turned toward Zoe's hot chocolate and began to stir it aggressively, showing indifference to Jules. "I am not sure yet."

Jules noticed Angela's evasiveness and took a new tactic, en-gaging Bernard instead. "Bernard, have you ever skied Mürren? It's a nice place. We should go there someday while Angela is here."

Bernard looked up and said, "No, I haven't skied it – but would like to someday. Angela, see that over there? That's Mürren. See those slopes? Would you like to go later this week?"

"Sure," she said with little emotion. She stared at him. Bernard caught the accusatory glance and smiled back.

Food came, and they dug into their plates. They poured white wine liberally into each other's glasses. Zoe's legs dangled back and forth contently from her chair, monitoring the surrounding adults. Jules made sure everyone was taken care of. Angela annoyingly checked texts. Theo was slightly bent over, next to Bernard, a hand on his thigh. After lunch, Jules suggested they catch the train back up the mountain and ski down to Grindelwald.

At Kleine Scheidegg, they got out of the train, retrieved their skis, and lined up on the ridge overlooking the vast valley below. Bernard, sensing his daughter's annoyance, stood close to her and gave her a warm hug. She faked a smile.

Jules noticed Bernard's solicitous attention to Angela. She continued to be impressed by his thoughtfulness. It gave her great comfort. They all inched forward on the slope and skied to town.

The Deckers headed back to Bern, and Bernard and Angela walked back to their apartment. It had turned dark. Soft orange light spilled out of shops and houses onto the fresh snow.

"You're awfully quiet tonight," Bernard noted.

"Hmm." Angela responded without elaboration.

"What's up?"

Angela didn't respond at first, then hesitatingly began, "Is there something up between you and Theo?"

Bernard gulped. "Like what?" he replied, stalling for time to think of an answer.

"I don't know. You seem very close for having just met."

"He's a nice guy. We get along."

Angela, annoyed, pressed him. "Dad, the shirt I found last night, it's his."

Bernard put his hands in his coat pockets and stared at the ground before him. They continued to walk up the hill toward the apartment. He didn't respond.

"Dad?"

"It's complicated," he began tentatively.

They reached the front door and went into the apartment. Bernard hung his coat on the hook just inside. Angela took hers off and laid it on a stool near an easy chair where she sat down. Bernard turned on a table lamp and went to the fireplace to prepare a fire.

As he lit some kindling, he continued, "Angela, this is hard for me."

Angela sat with her arms crossed, waiting for him to continue.

"It all happened very quickly. Theo has feelings for me and, I guess, I'm not entirely unhappy about it."

"So, you're gay?"

"Honey, I don't know."

"Either you are or you're not."

"That's not really true. You should know that."

Angela continued to glare sternly at her father. Bernard remained facing the fireplace to avoid her gaze. Finally, he turned to her. "Sexuality is complicated."

"That's why mom left you, right?"

Bernard began to tremble, the sense of guilt and shame overtaking him. He wandered into the kitchen to pour himself a drink. "Do you want something to drink?"

"No."

He came back out into the living room area. "Yes, I guess I wasn't enough for your mom. She deserved more." Bernard struggled with whether to tell Angela the truth about Susan being a spy and marrying him for ulterior reasons. He realized if he told Angela, not only would she not believe him, but it might get Theo into trouble. And he didn't underestimate Susan's capacity to forge some kind of international intrigue that would land him in trouble as well. It was easier to just take the hit, assume responsibility, and move on. But it meant losing respect in her eyes.

"I always knew it."

"What, that I was gay?"

"No, that she just tolerated you. Now I know why."

Bernard felt horrible. He took another long sip of wine and

stuffed his feelings deep down into his gut. He felt himself tighten. "If it's any consolation, I was always faithful to your mother," Bernard added, hoping to elicit some sympathy.

"Below the surface, she always seemed unhappy," Angela noted defensively of her mom.

"Yes, she seemed that way. I hope she is happy now."

Angela twitched her head and turned away from Bernard's view. She knew her mom wasn't happy with Charles, but she was angry at her father and didn't want to concede an inch. "She is."

Bernard suspected she wasn't and knew Angela was angry at him. "I'm sorry our holiday is ending on such a sour note. I had hoped this would be an enjoyable time for you, for us."

"It was. I think I need to go out."

"I can understand. Do you want me to go with you, or do you just want to be alone?"

"Alone." Angela got up, put on her coat and hat, and said, "I'll be back later. Don't wait up."

"Be careful."

She walked out the door, closing it forcefully.

Bernard sat down on the sofa and sighed. A difficult conversation was over, and his daughter's anger was no longer in his face. But now he faced two more days of hostility until she returned home. He went back to the kitchen and cut a few slices of cheese and bread. He wasn't hungry, but he needed something to nibble on.

The next day he woke to find Angela had packed her bags and was sitting at the table sipping a cup of coffee. "Hey, dear, what's up?"

"I think I'm going to leave early. Felippe invited me to visit him in Bern."

"I'm sorry about last night. I'm sure you're disappointed."

"Hmm," she noted. She took another sip of coffee and then continued, "I'm sorry, too. I overreacted. You have a right to your life."

"I hope we can get past this. I'm so proud of you, and I don't want something coming between us."

Angela didn't look up. She kept looking at her phone and sipping coffee.

"Could I meet you for lunch in Bern tomorrow?"

Angela nodded.

"Do you have a place to stay?"

"Felippe suggested a hotel in the city. Why don't you text me? We can meet. I'm leaving the following day for Boston."

"Sounds good. Do you have enough money, tickets?"

"I'm all set."

Angela finished her breakfast, went one more time to the bathroom, and then put on her coat to go to the station. "Can I walk with you?" Bernard inquired.

She nodded. Bernard smiled contently and put on his coat, hat, and gloves. As they walked toward the station, Angela began, "Theo seems like a nice person, but I don't understand how you and he can do this to Jules and Zoe."

"We can talk about this tomorrow. Jules and Theo have a unique relationship, and she's very happy for him, for me. I'll explain."

As they got to the station, the announcement for boarding was being made. Bernard and Angela embraced. She stepped into the carriage, placed her bags in the storage area, took a seat, and waved to her father as the train quietly pulled out of the station. He turned and walked slowly back into town and toward his apartment, where he planned to just read and relax by the fire, processing everything that had transpired.

8

Chapter Eight

A few days later, Bernard rose early and fixed a cup of coffee. Faint light rose over the highest peaks, eating away at the blue indigo night sky. Angela should have arrived in Boston, and he waited anxiously for a text. Their meeting the day before in Bern had not gone well. She had been relentless in her anger, blaming him for her parents' divorce and accusing him of sabotaging Jules's and Theo's marriage as well. He imagined Susan welcoming the information, more cover for her deception.

Bernard felt a wave of resentment surge through him. The wound of Susan's betrayal festered with the new realization that he had lost his daughter's respect. He wondered if he should confront his ex- and explain things to Angela. He rehearsed the idea in his head and concluded it could only make things worse. Susan was a force to contend with, and Bernard knew she would do anything to preserve her work and the life she had created for herself. The only consolation was that karma might catch up with her. In the meantime, he would just have to bear the consequences and make the best of his time in Grindelwald.

He glanced out the window and noticed a trail leading from the back of the apartment up the hill. He thought a day on snowshoes might be an antidote to his malaise. He remembered seeing some equipment in the hall closet and went to check. Amidst brooms, cleaning supplies, and rags, he found a shiny pair of aluminum snowshoes hanging on the wall. He pulled them out and noticed they were in good shape with quick release belts and fasteners. He took a shower and dressed. He laid out the map of the town on the dining table and considered various routes. One ascended from his complex through a thick forest toward the Bort guesthouse and restaurant. He thought it might be a pleasant treat to walk up, have lunch, and then take the gondola back down.

The surface of the trail was frosty from the cold overnight. The cleats gripped the hard surface, and he made good time. He stopped every fifteen minutes to catch his breath and take in the scenery. The lower part of the trail traversed snow-covered pastures and wooden barns. The trail narrowed and hugged a rocky ridge enshrouded in early morning shadows. Tall pines clung to the steep slope, their boughs shedding fine snow as the wind gently blew over them.

Bernard rounded a corner where the narrow hiking path joined one of the ski trails. He walked along the side of the groomed piste, digging his poles into the soft snow, his wide snowshoes keeping him secure on the surface. The sun had just risen over the Wetterhorn, and he felt its warmth on his face. It felt good to get out and walk, to clear his head. In the pristine alpine air and snow, the events of the past few days felt less overwhelming.

The first clumsy attempts at affection with Theo seemed distant and surreal. Had they really taken place? Was it all a mirage that would evaporate as he stepped forward? His life with Susan and Angela – even broken as it was - seemed more solid with the tangibles of home, daughter, and friends. He would return to Boston where the practicalities of life would anchor his future, not an ethereal, handsome Swiss politician from Bern.

He continued his climb. It became warm. He pulled off his jacket and wrapped it around his waist. He zipped his cap into a pocket and pulled out sunglasses to shield his eyes from the bright reflection off the snow. His lungs filled with clean air, and even though his legs burned with the exertion of his climb, he felt strong and in good shape.

He chuckled at the surprises life had tossed at him. He wondered if he had always been gay. Had there been clues he overlooked such as chaste relationships with high-school girlfriends, muscling up in college, or the fascination with handsome Italian waiters in Boston's North End – an interest he always chalked up as a matter of language, not something more physical, raw, primal. He laughed at picking out scarves with Susan and fussing over the placement of furniture in their home. He wondered if she knew under the surface. Had this made it easier for her to keep her emotional distance, not really investing in their relationship?

He considered the word 'gay.' How odd to think it described him? Was that really his tribe? Maybe he was just sexually fluid or bi-sexual. He enjoyed kissing Theo, but he was anxious about the next steps, the more serious expressions of love and passion. What would that involve, and would he find it troubling, even disturbing?

He thought of Theo's body - solid, muscular, imposing – expressing sensitivity, tenderness, and affection. How deeply ingrained are our cultural biases, finding such a combination unnatural, unreal, atypical? Was he misreading Theo? Would he relax his heart and emotions only to find Theo was experimenting, playing around, ready to retreat to his safe diplomatic world and conventional family?

He was grateful that Bort came into view about 100 meters up

CROSSING BORDERS - 115

the trail. He was thirsty and ready for an early lunch. He finished the climb, got a table, and settled in for a relaxing break. The morning mist had burned away, leaving unobstructed views of the surrounding mountains and valleys. After placing his order, a text came in from Theo. He was on a trip to eastern Europe.

"Hi handsome! Are you free this evening for dinner? I'm flying home. Jules, Zoe, and I?"

He was surprised but giddy that Theo looked forward to seeing him. Tempering his enthusiasm with a bit of humor, he texted back, "*Et alors?*"

There was a pause. Bernard worried Theo might be annoyed. Finally, a text came in. "Is that a yes?"

"Of course." He wanted to type something a little more forward but wasn't sure what the protocol was yet with texting diplomats.

"Kruez und Post at 7 okay?"

"Perfect," he replied. "See you then." He then texted a photo of the view from his table.

Another text came in, "Have some profiteroles for me." Bernard glanced down at the stack of chocolate-covered pastries before him. How did he know?

Later that evening, Bernard strolled through town to the restaurant. It was cold, and light ice crystals formed in the frosty air. People were arm in arm, bundled up as they made their way to dinners or back home from shops. A slick coating of snow gathered on the pavement. Bernard was relieved to reach the hotel and the comforting warmth inside the restaurant.

Theo, Jules, and Zoe were seated at a corner booth in the front room. They had already ordered drinks when he hung his coat and snuggled up next to Jules on the banquette. Theo and Zoe were seated on the other side of the corner table. Small candles in star-shaped holders twinkled golden light on the red tablecloth. Jules kissed him warmly on the cheeks. He stood up and walked toward

Zoe and Theo, giving them each a warm set of kisses as well. He and Theo exchanged a protracted glance.

"So, how was your week, Bernard?" Jules began.

"Not so good. Things didn't go well with Angela." Zoe looked up, surprised. "I just don't understand. Most young people are more open-minded."

Jules leaned over and began in a softer voice, "If I might interject. It's not about your being gay. It's that the image she had of her family, of you and Susan, has been shattered. She doesn't know how to make sense of it all, and she doesn't have all the information. She's rightfully confused."

Bernard looked over at Theo, assuring him he was firm in his intent to preserve confidentiality and not say anything openly about Susan's work. But he wondered what Theo had shared with Jules.

Jules continued, "It's very courageous to assume responsibility when someone else is really to blame. Eventually, your daughter will come around."

"Perhaps. I hope so."

Zoe reached over and touched Bernard's hand, offering him a sip of her hot chocolate.

"Thank you, Zoe. You're always so kind."

Theo and Jules both looked proudly at her.

They ordered entrees and continued to share stories of the week. Zoe had won a prize at school. Jules closed on several proposals with clients, and Theo convinced several eastern European counterparts to collaborate on new green infrastructure work. Everyone's success made Bernard more self-conscious of his own precarious situation. He tried to shake it off, reminding himself that few people have the luxury of spending two months in Switzerland trying to find themselves.

Jules hadn't changed out of her work clothes. Bernard could see why the men in her office were intimidated. She struck a daunting pose – with high heels, a tight-fitting dress, a gray-blue vest, and a turquoise scarf. He still found her sensual and alluring. He wondered if he had been wrong after all. Was he attracted to her instead of Theo? But as he considered that thought, he glanced over at Theo, and his heart fluttered. Theo looked up and caught his eye. He was certain of his affections.

Toward the end of dinner, Jules leaned over to Zoe and asked, "Do you mind if you and I have a sleepover tonight and let your dad and Bernard have a sleepover at Bernard's place? It can be girls' night out?"

Zoe beamed with delight and nodded yes.

Bernard gave Theo a surprised and inquisitive look. Theo then added, "Jules and I discussed it. We don't want you to be alone." As he said that, he looked at Zoe.

Bernard recognized the framing of this was done to protect Zoe from what was developing between him and her father. Bernard wondered, however, if she wasn't more aware of the situation than her parents were willing to admit.

Bernard looked over at Jules and asked, "You okay?"

She placed her hand on his leg. "Absolutely. Zoe and I will have a fun time. We'll meet you guys for skiing tomorrow."

They retrieved their coats, walked out into the winter night air, and exchanged warm kisses and hugs as they went their separate ways.

Bernard was quiet and anxious as they walked home. The initial intensity and allure of the last weekend was remote and dreamlike. He wondered if he was making a mistake. Theo felt more like a new acquaintance, not a lover he was leading home to his bed. They were both deep in thought, distant, hesitant.

Theo detected Bernard's reticence. "Are you okay with this?"

"Yeah, sure," he tried to sound convincing.

"I thought about you all week," Theo assured him.

"Me, too."

They arrived at the door, Bernard fumbled for the keys, and let them in. He wanted Theo to take the lead, pull him close, give him a kiss. Instead, Theo hung up his coat and walked into the living area as if seeing it for the first time. Bernard sensed something wasn't right, that perhaps Theo had second thoughts, too.

"Can I get you a drink? Brandy, wine?"

"Wine would be great."

"Can you get a fire started?" he inquired of Theo, hoping to re-focus his attention.

"Sure." Theo walked over to the fireplace, put some kindling under some fresh logs, and lit the fire. Yellow flames began licking at the rough bark.

Bernard came back with a bottle of wine and two glasses. He set them on a side table, poured the wine into the glasses, and sat on the sofa next to Theo, handing him a glass. They toasted and took a drink.

After a prolonged silence, Bernard began, "This seems awkward."

"I know," Theo said in return, visibly relieved that the ice had been broken.

"Why do you think so?"

"Maybe it's the reality of it all. Last weekend we were play-ing, caught up in the moment. Now it seems more intentional, calculated."

"Yeah, that makes sense. I have to say I was surprised when Jules said what she did."

"You mean about a sleepover?"

"Yes."

"Sorry if we caught you off guard. It made sense when we discussed it. It doesn't seem that way now."

Bernard took another sip of wine. He expected Theo to tell him he was going to go home after all. He glanced over at him and

noticed his eyes were watering. Maybe he had regrets or felt conflicted over being with a man. He never imagined such an imposing
man could be so emotional. It surprised him. He felt less awkward.
He was eager to console Theo.

Surprising himself, he leaned over onto Theo's solid body. It felt
warm, strong, and soft. He held Theo's face in his hands and pulled
it close to his, giving him a generous, moist kiss. Theo kissed him
back, rubbing Bernard's shoulders.

Theo sighed and whispered, "That feels better." The contact of
their bodies dissipated their anxiety.

Bernard felt more relaxed. Theo smiled and reached for his hand.
They sat facing each other for a few moments and then Theo slid
his hand over the bottom of Bernard's sweater and lifted it. Bernard
pulled out his arms and tucked his head as Theo pulled the sweater
up over his head. He massaged Bernard's chest, warm and firm.

Theo unzipped his own sweater and pulled it off. He then
kneeled on the sofa, lifting his arms so that Bernard could reach
over and pull off his tee shirt. Bernard wrapped his hands around
Theo's muscular torso and slid his hands up, bringing the shirt off
with them. Their bodies glowed in the soft light of the fire. Theo
pushed Bernard back onto the sofa and reclined on him.

Bernard began to shake. He told himself, 'Relax, this is okay.' But
his body had its own mind, feeling tense and anxious, continuing
to shake. Theo felt it. He didn't know what to do. Would it pass, or
was this too traumatic for Bernard? "Are you okay?" he asked.

Bernard nodded no. Then he whispered, "I think it might be
better if I hold you instead."

Theo rolled over, and Bernard placed his leg over Theo's, stroking
his hairy chest and feeling the contours of his pecs. He didn't know
what possessed him, but he leaned over and began to kiss Theo's
abdomen, drifting down toward his belt. It felt oddly natural.

Theo pulled Bernard on top of him and rubbed his back. At

first Bernard shook, then he relaxed. They kissed. Theo held Bernard tightly and rolled them both over so that Theo was now on top. He didn't let go of the tight grip, hoping to prevent Bernard's body from trembling. At first Bernard felt a tremor but, then nothing, just the security of Theo's embrace.

It dawned on Theo that this really was Bernard's first time with a man. He had a new appreciation for his vulnerability. He loosened his hold and Bernard remained relaxed, calm.

Bernard was relieved that he had ceased to shake and now felt the full intensity of Theo's body on top of him. Theo looked down at him, taking a read. Bernard whispered, "You feel good."

"Is it okay if I stay over?"

Bernard nodded.

"You sure?"

"Yes. But you brought nothing with you."

"You mean like pajamas?"

Bernard nodded.

"I'm traveling light," he said, winking at Bernard.

Theo got up, took Bernard's hand, and led him into the bedroom. They stood awkwardly at the edge of the bed. Theo then said, "Do you mind if I use the bathroom?"

"No - and use whatever you need in there."

Theo smiled and walked down the hall. Bernard made a quick inventory of the room. Should he leave on a soft light, turn it off, pull back the covers, pull out some shorts to wear? Before he could decide, Theo was back in the room. "I'll be right back," Bernard said as he walked down the hall himself.

When he came back, Theo was in bed under the covers. Bernard turned off the lamp. An orange light streamed through the window from an adjoining building. Bernard took off his pants but left on his undershorts. He climbed into bed with Theo.

At first, he laid next to Theo on his back, not sure what to do.

Theo had on his undershorts as well. Theo leaned toward him and said, "You are so handsome."

Bernard smiled. "You, too." He reached his arm around Theo's back and pulled him on top of him. He was relieved that he didn't shake. He savored the full weight of Theo's body on him, Theo's hardness pressing against his own.

Bernard reached around Theo's back and slipped his hands down over his buttocks under his shorts. They were full, round, and firm. He slipped the shorts off. Theo then reached down and pulled Bernard's off. They laid on their sides facing each other, feeling the warm hardness pressed against each other.

They fumbled around, felt each other, and kissed. Theo pushed himself up against Bernard, wrapping his legs around him. They held each other; their bodies entwined like roots of a tree. They rolled back and forth, neither making a definitive move to bring things to a climax. Theo was afraid to push Bernard too quickly, and Bernard felt inexperienced, unwilling to take any further initiatives. "Et alors?" Bernard interjected with humor.

Theo laughed, rolling over on his back. Bernard climbed up over him, bracing himself on his elbows over Theo. He made an inquisitive face, and Theo laughed again.

"What's so funny?" Bernard inquired.

"Us."

"How so?"

"I feel like a teenager."

"I never did this in my teens."

"Me either, although if Sebastian in the gymnasium had made a pass, I would have gladly succumbed."

"I assume he never did."

"Unfortunately, no. But this is better. You look a little like him, English features with a touch of Mediterranean color and dark eyes.

But this," Theo reached down and held Bernard, "is much more impressive than what I saw in the locker room showers."

Bernard blushed and stiffened more, brushing his hand slowly over Theo's erection. He ran his hand over Theo's thigh and then slid it between his legs, amazed at the physical and emotional intimacy of the moment and the capacity of people to share themselves so deeply through touch. Each shed his guard and felt the raw presence of the other. They leaned into each other, opened their mouths, and breathed each other in.

Theo got up and straddled Bernard, kneeling just over Bernard's erection, increasing in hardness. He rubbed his hands under Bernard's balls, feeling the moistness of his skin and the pulses of heat rising from deep within as he massaged him. Bernard arched his back and moaned, looking up at Theo towering over him. He reached up and rubbed his hands over Theo's chest, muscles tensing with desire.

Theo spit in his hand and grabbed Bernard's hard shaft, giving it long, tender strokes. Bernard squirmed in pleasure and spread his legs slightly. Theo angled his own erection close by and then took both their engorged cocks in his large hand, rubbing them together. Bernard placed his hands behind Theo's upper legs, feeling them flex as Theo continued to stroke them both. He continued to run his hands up Theo's firm buttocks, moist with sweat and quivering with anticipation.

Theo's chest became red, and his pecs tightened as he became increasingly aroused. "You are so sexy," he whispered to Bernard, gazing down at his deep brown eyes. He continued to massage their erections enfolded in his hands, heat increasing as they slid back and forth against each other.

Bernard could feel pulses of pleasure rise from the base of his shaft and, suddenly, he exploded in Theo's hand. He gazed at Theo,

who flexed his lower abdomen and stretched his own erection upward, erupting in spasms of release as well.

Theo collapsed onto Bernard's chest. Theo rested his head near
Bernard's heart, listening to it pound rapidly and eventually return
to a normal pace. Bernard kissed the side of Theo's neck, breathing
in the scent of his body.

Theo lifted his head and smiled warmly at Bernard, giving him
a warm kiss. He rolled off and went to the bathroom. Bernard
followed a few minutes later and approached him from behind,
holding him tenderly, both looking into the mirror. They said nothing but smiled contently. They returned to bed and fell soundly to
sleep, pressed close to each other.

The next morning, Bernard slipped out of bed, put on shorts and
a tee shirt, and made coffee in the kitchen. He set out bread, jam,
and muesli. Theo walked in shortly after, wearing only his shorts. In
the morning light, the proportions of Theo's body were fully apparent. His tousled dark blond hair complemented darker chest hair
and a stubble beard. Bernard handed him a steaming cup of coffee.

"Hey handsome," Theo began, stroking his hand over Bernard's
back and then around over his pecs. Bernard felt himself get hard.
He looked down at Theo, noticing the same reaction.

"How did you sleep?" Bernard inquired.

"Like never before."

"Hmm," Bernard moaned. "Help yourself," he pointed to the table.

They both sat down and began to eat. Bernard inquired, "Are we
meeting Jules and Zoe today?"

"Are you up for it?"

"Yes. I think it would be good."

The reality of the situation hit Bernard. He felt guilty, anxious,
concerned. He had slept with a man he hardly knew and had done
so with the blessing of his wife. What kind of weird parallel uni-
verse had he stepped into? Theo seemed unfazed by it all. Perhaps

he had looked forward to such an eventuality, living many years as a frustrated gay man in a straight marriage. For Bernard, everything was new, most importantly his own new self-awareness.

Theo went home to clean up and get his ski gear while Bernard took a shower and dressed for the day. A few moments later, Theo texted, "Change of plans. I need to take care of some things at home."

"Everything okay?" Bernard texted back anxiously.

"Yes, Jules is just not feeling well. I'll touch base with you later. Why don't you go ahead and ski on your own?"

Bernard felt faint and sat down, hanging his head low between his knees. He let the sensation pass, stood up, and drank a glass of water. He had no interest in skiing, dreading Jules's and Theo's change of heart. He pondered whether to call, to text, to offer help, but decided it was best to stay out of the way and wait for the outcome – whatever that might be.

A few hours passed, and he hadn't heard from Theo. He became even more preoccupied, convinced Jules was not okay and that she and Theo were rethinking things. What had he been thinking? It was all so bizarre. Maybe Angela was right – that he had come between them.

He laid down on the sofa and closed his eyes, hoping to wake up and realize all of this was a strange dream. He woke later, the apartment dark, the nightmare real. He looked at his watch. It was six PM. He looked at his phone – no texts or email from Theo. He went into the kitchen and fixed a salad and poured a glass of wine. He sat at the table, staring out into the night. The next thing he knew, it was 1 AM, and he had fallen asleep on the table. He shuffled down the hall, and without taking off his clothes, fell into bed.

9

Chapter Nine

Bernard woke the next day feeling the full import of Theo's silence, the disappointment of being ignored, and the inevitable questioning of his perceptions - how naïve and gullible he had been. He took another look at his phone but already knew there would be no messages. He couldn't eat and had no interest in skiing. He pulled up an electronic map of Switzerland on his computer, searching for a place to travel, to get out of town, clear his head, think things through.

He thought about Geneva, Freiburg, and Basel, but he kept gravitating to Zurich. He hadn't been in some time, and always liked the old historic part of town. He was also curious. There was a large gay population in the city, and he thought it might be time to sort through new feelings and insights about himself.

He packed a small travel bag and put on a pair of jeans, a sweater, and a dark overcoat. It felt good to shed the ski outfit and blend in with the general population. He worried that his continued time in Grindelwald might be fraught with tension, hoping to avoid running into Theo or Jules. The ride out of town and through the canyon toward Interlaken felt cathartic, even if unnerving, as if he was escaping from a terrible nightmare.

In Bern, he connected to the fast train to Zurich. He was amazed at how smooth and quiet the train was as it swiftly passed snow covered farmland and small villages. A couple of hours after he had left Grindelwald, he pulled into the Zurich station.

It was massive - a maze of tracks, underground galleries, and shops. He had booked a room in a small hotel in the old part of the city. He walked through the downtown section of Zurich past large department stores and then made his way toward the river. He crossed one of the bridges and wound his way up the hill of narrow stone pedestrian ways and charming historic buildings.

He found the address and walked inside the lobby of a boutique inn. A distinguished elderly man greeted him, took down his personal information and gave him a key, saying, "We hope you will have a pleasant stay with us. Your room is on the third floor with marvelous views of the city and the lake. If there's anything you need, just let us know."

"Well, there is one question I have. Are there some nice jazz or music clubs in the area you might recommend?"

The man winked at him and said, "It depends on what you have in mind."

Bernard blushed, not knowing how to respond.

The man ran his eyes up and down Bernard and said, "Hm. I think I know the right place. There's a small venue just a few blocks around the corner. A local hangout – a more mature crowd, and they have a nice female vocalist who performs nightly."

"Sounds perfect."

"Tell Deirdre that Jonathan sent you. She'll find you a place."

"Thank you."

Bernard climbed the antique staircase and opened the door to his room. It was small but classy. Large windows faced the river, the lake, and the skyline of Zurich. The Grossmünster church loomed nearby, dusted with fresh snow that had fallen the night before. Most thought of Zurich as a sterile and cold business center, but the city was more beautiful and charming than Bernard had imagined, with the well-preserved medieval district spread out before him. In the distance, the Alps rose majestically in the haze.

Bernard unpacked, took a quick nap, and then went out shopping. The neighborhood was a maze of cobblestone squares lined with cafes, restaurants, and specialty boutiques. He picked up some clothes at a few men's shops and some novels at a small, independent bookstore. He enjoyed the feel of printed books, and being in Zurich, he could find novels in German and French.

He found a quiet bistro for dinner. While eating, he looked up the name of the club the hotel had recommended, "Chez Nous." The review said: "Quiet, friendly neighborhood gay hangout. Mature but good-looking crowd. Classy vocalists and live music. Generous drinks."

Bernard had only been to a gay bar a few times with friends in New Haven and Boston. The idea of going in alone was frightening, but he felt it might be the only way to make sense out of the last few days. Was he just into Theo or was this something bigger, a new self-awareness and identity?

He found the club, a traditional pub-looking venue with a dark wood panel façade and leaded windows. He pushed open the door and a woman, or at least he thought she was, greeted him. She looked at him carefully and Bernard said, "Are you Deirdre? Jonathan sent me."

In a deep masculine voice, Deirdre replied, "Welcome, honey. Let me take your coat. Make yourself at home." She took his coat, handed him a receipt, and pointed inside the room.

Bernard felt many heads turn toward him from the long antique bar just inside the door. He wanted to grab his coat and run. In-stead, he took one step, then another – just like skiing, he thought to himself – just keep pushing forward.

There were some high-top tables scattered about the room and a brightly lit stage where a woman was singing a sultry jazz piece accompanied by a man on the piano. She was dressed in a long, low-cut sparkly gown, and the accompanist wore a classic tux. Bernard spotted an empty table, lifted himself onto the stool, and leaned nervously on his elbows.

He surveyed the room as imperceptibly as possible. A cute buff waiter approached from behind and began, "It's a slow start. I know. Trust me, it will get better later. What would you like to drink, dear?"

"I'll have a brandy, straight up."

"I'll be right back."

Bernard's first instinct was to check his phone, a convenient way to avoid the awkwardness of sitting alone. Another high-top opened along the wall, so he moved over, feeling less exposed, more concealed.

The waiter returned with his drink, giving him a warm smile as he left. The vocalist was good, and Bernard listened attentively.

People trickled in, and the club filled, people now standing in clusters around the intimate hall. The sound level increased as friends spoke over the music. Five men squeezed into an open space near Bernard's table, nodding an implicit 'hello' and 'we will respect your privacy' to him as they huddled together.

Bernard nodded back, grateful for their warmth. One of the five glanced back at Bernard over his shoulder. He looked like he was in his late 40s or early 50s, medium height, trim, short brown hair, and large expressive eyes.

An older gentleman wandered from the bar and leaned against the wall near Bernard's table, watching the vocalist but glancing at

Bernard from time to time. He looked French, with dark hair, a prominent nose, and an angular face. He looked good for his age, but Bernard didn't feel any attraction to him. Gratefully, the man never approached.

Bernard wasn't sure what he hoped to accomplish, and he almost got up and left. The music was good, but he really didn't want to meet anyone, fearing that it might lead to other expectations which he clearly had no intention of satisfying. The young man in the group of five kept glancing back at Bernard, and Bernard smiled. The guy nodded, excused himself from his friends, and walked toward Bernard.

"Hello, I'm Stephan."

"Bernard," he replied. "Nice to meet you."

"Can I get you a drink?" Stephan offered, looking at Bernard's nearly empty glass.

Bernard hesitated and Stephan interjected, "Not a problem, if no."

"No, no, that's very generous of you. I'll have a brandy – straight up."

Stephan waved down the waiter, who took his order.

"Are you visiting from out of town?"

Bernard realized most people in the club were local and he must have stood out. "Yes, I'm visiting from the States."

"Business?"

"No, I'm here on vacation."

"You came to Zurich in the winter on vacation?"

"No, I was skiing – or, I should say, I am skiing but just came to the city for a quick visit."

The drinks came, and Stephan raised his glass to Bernard's, "*Salute.*"

Bernard continued, "She's a talented singer," glancing toward the stage.

"Yes, Miriam is quite good." He took a sip of his drink and then leaned closer to Bernard. "So – you're a skier. Where are you skiing?"

"Grindelwald."

"That's a nice place."

"Do you ski?"

"I used to, but I had an accident. I usually go to Spain for winter vacation."

Bernard felt the conversation wasn't going anywhere and, even though Stephan was friendly and nice looking, they didn't seem to have any chemistry. One of his friends came over, placed his arm on Stephan's shoulder, and whispered something to him.

"Do you want to join us?" Stephan invited Bernard.

"Sure, that would be nice."

Stephan led Bernard to his group of friends, introduced them, and then whispered in Bernard's ear, "You're very cute, you know."

"Hmm," he managed to sigh ever so tentatively. "You are, too – and you have a nice group of friends."

"Be careful. They're not as nice as they seem."

"And you?" Bernard interjected.

"Oh, I'm an angel!" he grinned sheepishly.

Bernard then rubbed his hand over Stephan's shoulder and said, "I don't feel any wings."

"They're someplace else," he said playfully as he winked.

Bernard felt like he was on an icy ski run with no way to stop. What had possessed him to interject a provocative open-ended comment like that? Where had it come from? He never had an exchange like that before, and he felt it was going to end badly. 'How do I stop this?' he asked himself.

Stephan must have read Bernard's reticence all over his face and toned things down. "Are you here for a few days?"

"Just an overnight."

"Well, I'll have to work quickly, then."

Bernard laughed but said nothing back.

"You okay?" Stephan inquired, noting Bernard's continued hesitancy.

Bernard paused and then just blurted out, "I'm a little nervous. This is my first time in a gay bar."

Stephan was, at first, speechless. Then he said, "Whoa – sorry I was coming on so strong."

"It's okay. You're cute and disarming – not like some of those over there who would have made me very uneasy."

"Yes, that's a scary crowd." They both looked at the bar and laughed.

"I'm sorry I'm such a bore," Bernard interjected.

"That's not what I picked up. In fact, you're quite funny!"

"Funny?"

"Well, also cute, alluring, mysterious," Stephan continued.

"Hmm."

"Let's go back to your table and talk."

"That would be nice," Bernard replied.

They sat, and Stephan began, "So, why now? What led you to come to a gay bar at this time in your life?"

"You mean so late in life?"

"No, I didn't say that – remember, you're cute!" Stephan said, placing his hand on Bernard's forearm.

Bernard blushed. "Well, it's complicated."

"Usually is. Spill."

"I met someone on the slopes – but he's married."

"To a woman?"

"Yes."

"Those closeted straight men – always a problem."

"That was me – at least until my wife left me last year," Bernard explained.

"The perfect storm." Stephan took a dramatic sip of his drink. "Continue dear."

"Well, this guy came on strong – and his wife seemed cool with it."

"But, in the end, she wasn't," Stephan raised his brows.

"Right."

"Poor guy. You're going to need another drink." Stephan waved to the waiter for another round.

"But the experience helped me realize that I was probably gay all along – so, in some respects, I'm grateful. But it's still a bummer."

"So, you came to Chez Nous to confirm if you're gay?"

"Well, yes - well, not exactly."

"Um-hum. And how's that going for you?"

"Well, I don't know. What do you think?"

Stephan scanned Bernard's body and declared, "I'd say you're a certifiable poufter."

"Relieved!" Bernard interjected humorously.

"In all seriousness, you're a natural. You seemed like you fit in earlier – and you certainly kept your cool during our little banter back there."

"I don't know where that came from."

"It's a gift – genetic."

Bernard grinned. "And you?"

"*Moi* – well dear, that's a tortuous story."

"I'm all ears."

"Short version – I was thrown out of the house by my conservative parents, picked up by a conscientious social worker, and met my first boyfriend in college – both of us studying history."

"Wow, that's quite a journey. So, do you teach?"

"Yes."

"And boyfriend?"

"Just coming out of a long-term relationship, so I'm on the prowl."

"So, how do you know?"

"Know you're gay?"

"Um-hum."

Stephan paused, looking thoughtful, and then said, "Let me be serious – although it's not my nature. There are all kinds of signs – some people talk about an aesthetic sensibility, others a flair for the dramatic, and some an attraction to gender non-conforming behavior. For me, the telltale sign is the flutter in your stomach. Most of us can find certain women attractive, even feel an emotional attachment to them, but it is that deep flutter in the pit of your stomach that says it all. When you feel you are losing control of yourself, are riding a tidal wave of attraction to someone and, when you see them, you feel it deep within yourself – then you know," Stephan explained.

He paused, took a sip of his drink and then continued, "Most of us have been taught to fear and control those feelings – as if they are impure, beastly, and sinful. They are our body's way of drawing us toward others, of connecting on a deep, loving level. They are an original blessing – not a problem. Once you accept that and begin to pay attention, not only will you know who you are, but you will be guided in choices about people — kind of like intuition."

"But how is that different from lust? Don't we all get a flutter in our stomach when we see a beautiful body?" Bernard asked.

"Yes – and we should not shame that. It is part of who we are — a gift. We don't have to act on those desires – just accept them and ask what they are trying to tell us. If you're in a relationship and you see an attractive person, it might be a message that your relationship isn't that good, or that you need to pay more attention to your relationship, or simply that there's lots of eye candy out there. You'll know when you ask yourself, 'what is the message here?' But if you shame the feelings or desires, you can't ask what they mean."

"Wow," Bernard responded. "I had no idea."

Stephan smiled. "I know. I look pretty shallow, right?"

"I didn't say that. It's just I've never heard anyone express that so succinctly."

"I've learned a lot in the school of life – and happened to have taken a cool course at the university a while back."

Stephan lifted his hand and took a long sip of his drink. "And – so?"

Bernard thought to himself, '*et alors?*' – and chuckled.

"What's so funny?"

"Oh, an expression – when you said – 'and so' – it made me think."

"And so – who makes you flutter?"

"He does – my married skier friend."

"What's the message?"

"The first one is that I'm a certified poufter – as you said."

"Bravo! I had no doubt."

"The second is that I love him."

"That's going to be tough."

"But if the flutter is part of our deepest self – who's saying it isn't a message that is coming from something greater – an invitation to reach out?"

"Now you're scaring me," Stefan exclaimed.

"No, really. Maybe it's a message for both of us – and we have to take it where it leads us."

"But what if that is just to lead you to a new self-awareness?"

"I feel like it's more. I think I overreacted. I need to see it through."

"What does that mean? I don't get to take you home tonight?" Stephan implored with sad eyes and pouty lips.

"Stephan, as tempting as it is, probably not."

"Probably – you mean there's a chance?" his eyes opening wide.

"No, that was just a polite let down. I have to go."

"Not without a kiss." Stephan reached over and pulled Bernard close to him and gave him a warm, wet, generous kiss. Bernard kissed back, savoring the *mélange* of alcohol and Stephan's breath – sweet and earthy.

They hugged. Stephan pulled a piece of paper out of his pocket and jotted down his cell number. "Call if you're back in Zurich and a free agent."

Bernard chuckled. He ceremoniously kissed the piece of paper and slipped it into his front pocket. He smiled warmly and headed toward the door of the bar.

"You leaving so early, dear?" Deirdre stated, grabbing his coat.

"Sorry to say I have someone I need to check in on."

"Be safe!"

Bernard stepped out into the cold, damp night air and made his way back to the inn. It was late, so he undressed and slipped under the puffy down cover and fell into a peaceful sleep.

The following morning, he was eager to return to Grindelwald. He walked to the train station and bought a ticket, boarding the first leg to Bern. As he was walking along the platform, he saw Theo entering two cars up. He was accompanied by a younger man, both dressed for work. The young man was affable, grinning, and had grabbed Theo's elbow as they climbed aboard.

Bernard felt his heart stop briefly and wondered what to do. His first instinct was to find a quiet, out of the way seat, and avoid any contact. His second was to walk forward and, in the search of a seat, run into them as if by accident. He settled for the first, found a seat, and slumped down low to avoid any accidental notice. His heart was filling with adrenaline, racing faster and faster. He took a couple of deep breaths and calmed down.

Although he presumed the man was a business colleague, they were boarding a train early in the morning, and it meant Theo had spent the night in Zurich. Was this another liaison under the guise of work, or was it all innocent? If innocent, why hadn't Theo let Bernard know?

Bernard stewed on his thoughts for the next hour as the train made its way to Bern. The closer to Bern, the more conflicted he felt. Should he follow them, bump into them, or just make his connection and continue to Grindelwald?

The conductor announced the arrival in Bern, and Bernard decided to follow Theo. Theo and his companion stepped onto the platform and headed to the main section of the station. Bernard waited for them to pass and trailed them. They exited in the direction of the government area of town. They stopped at a small café, went in, and began ordering coffee and pastry. Bernard reprimanded himself, 'this is crazy – just let it go.'

But he entered a café across the street and sat at a booth near the window and waited. About 30 minutes later, they exited. It had begun to rain, and the young man held Theo's arm as they both huddled under Theo's umbrella. 'They seem awfully chummy,' Theo remarked to himself.

They entered one of the main administrative buildings, and Bernard decided to continue his journey. He walked back to the station and boarded the next train to Interlaken. On board, he finally got a text from Theo.

"Hey there, sorry for the delay. I'm sure you're worried. Jules had to go to the hospital, and I had to make a trip to Zurich."

'Well,' Bernard thought to himself, 'at least the story seems plausible and consistent.' He wondered if he should text back – ask about Jules. He waited and decided not to respond right away.

Who was Theo's companion, and why hadn't Theo been in touch? It would have been so easy for him to just say hello. Sorry, I'm busy. Jules is ill. What did his silence suggest? Where would that leave him in the long term?

As the train got closer to Interlaken, the rain changed to a wet snow. Only the bases of the mountains were visible and, even as they made their way from Interlaken to Grindelwald, the fog and clouds were dense.

Once in town, he walked to his apartment and made a sandwich for lunch. He sat in the living room, watching the snow outside, and typed a text.

"Theo, good to hear from you. Sorry Jules is ill. I hope she's better. Let me know if there's anything I can do."

No reprimand, questions, or elaboration – just a quick, straight-forward response.

"Thanks for your understanding. Jules is better," Theo responded, also without elaboration.

Bernard now became angry. This wasn't the kind of exchange two people would have who had such a strong connection.

"What's up?" he texted – not '*et alors*' – nor anything more significant – just an opening, an opportunity for Theo to explain.

Initially, there wasn't a response, then Theo texted: "We need to talk. Where are you?"

Bernard wanted to reply – 'where are you?' – but fought the urge. "At home."

"Meet you for dinner?"

"Sure. Where?"

"The brasserie?"

"In Bern?"

"No, there's one in Grindelwald, on Hornweg Strasse. 6 PM?"

"Sure, see you then."

Later, Bernard pushed the frosty door of the brasserie open. He had never noticed the place, a small family-run restaurant off the beaten path. A friendly woman greeted him and pointed out Theo, who was waiting nervously at a small table. Theo stood and embraced him tightly and kissed him on the cheeks. It was a good sign, Bernard thought to himself, but he remained on guard.

They sat. Theo poured Bernard a glass of wine and looked at him earnestly.

"Well?" Bernard began.

"I don't know how to put this delicately, so I'll just say it outright. Jules is pregnant."

"Pregnant?" Bernard exclaimed, blood rushing to his face.

"Yes, pregnant."

"How did this happen? When did this happen?"

Theo smiled nervously, looking down at the table where he was scratching his fingers on the soft wood tabletop. "She took a test the other day when she wasn't feeling well and had missed her period. Sure enough, the test was positive."

"You said she was in the hospital."

"She was nervous about her age and wanted to get things tested in case there were reasons to halt the pregnancy."

Bernard struggled with what to say and began, "How does that make you feel?"

"I'm happy but concerned. All of this," he said, gesturing at himself and Bernard, "and then that."

Bernard was annoyed at Theo's presumption that there was a 'this' after his lack of communication. All he could say was, "Hmm."

"She's very apologetic."

"Apologetic?" Bernard asked in disbelief.

"Yes, apologetic. She feels like this is going to ruin things for me, for us."

"But surely this is a big deal for the two of you. It can't not change things."

"Well, you're probably right."

"What do you mean, probably?"

"Well, Jules had some thoughts."

"And?"

"She wants to keep the baby. We've wanted Zoe to have a brother or sister."

Bernard smiled. "That's good."

"But get this. Jules suggested that you and I raise the baby."

"Whaaaat!" Bernard exclaimed. "You've got to be kidding."

"No, I was as surprised as you."

"What is she thinking?"

"She is afraid you and I will bond to the exclusion of her and Zoe, and she thinks if we raise the new baby, her baby, it will reinforce our connections – that is yours, mine, and hers."

"Theo, we have to talk. I don't know about this bonding thing you keep talking about."

"What do you mean?" Theo looked concerned.

"I mean, where were you the last few days? The last thing I heard from you was that Jules wasn't feeling well, that you had some things to deal with, and that I should go skiing the other day." Bernard felt himself get red in the face as he let out his disappointment and anger.

"But that's all I meant."

"Didn't you think I'd be anxious and concerned – not hearing from you for a couple of days?"

Theo looked down, aware of how he had hurt Bernard. "I'm sorry."

"Given what you were dealing with, I can understand, but I'm still upset."

"What do you mean, you're upset?"

"Precisely that, upset. We were having a good time, connecting, and then silence. I went crazy."

Theo creased his forehead. "Crazy?"

"Yes, crazy," Bernard repeated, becoming a little more relaxed.

"Well, is that a good thing?"

"Not if it happens again," he said, raising his eyebrows.

"I'm sorry."

"So, Jules wants us to raise the baby – that's very weird." Bernard creased his forehead and squinted his eyes in consternation.

"I know, it is rather unconventional, and I'm sure this is all moving quickly for you."

"That's for sure."

"What can I do?" Theo reached over for Bernard's hands, then pulled back, respecting what he imagined was a raw, tender moment for him.

Bernard paused, considered several responses, and then began, "I think we need to start over, lay cards on the table, and see if we are good."

"I can do that. How do we start?"

"I have to ask you – where were you this morning and who were you with?"

"What?"

"Just answer," Bernard stated emphatically.

"I was in Zurich, coming back from a late meeting the night before with representatives from the EU."

"And who were you with?"

"Jules's brother, François, who was at the meeting. Why?"

"I saw you. I was on the same train."

"Why didn't you say something to me?"

"What do you think? I don't hear from you, and you're boarding a morning train with an attractive guy. What would you conclude?"

"Probably the same. Sorry, but what were you doing in Zurich?"

"Finding myself."

"Elaborate."

"I needed to get away from here and went to Zurich. I went to a gay bar last night for the first time."

Theo smiled. "How was it?"

"What do you mean, how was it? You should be saying – I hope you didn't meet someone."

"Okay, I hope you didn't meet someone."

"I did. But it wasn't anything. We just had a philosophical conversation about being gay and coming out."

"Was he cute?"

"Yes, but he didn't make my heart flutter. You do." Bernard felt the sentiment too saccharine, but it was impossible to take it back.

Theo reached his hand over and put it on Bernard's. "I wish I could kiss you here."

"Me, too."

"Am I forgiven?" Theo looked imploringly at Bernard.

"We'll see."

"Are we okay?"

"I think so." Bernard smiled warmly.

"So, what's next?"

"Well – I'm not sure. We need to talk with Jules."

"She wants to talk with you. Are you free tomorrow for dinner? Our place?"

"Yeah, sure."

"In the meantime, do you have any plans?"

"I'll have to cancel a couple of dates I lined up but, but I think I can work you in. Are you free?"

"Of course."

They ordered their meals and caught up on news. When they finished, they put on their coats and stepped out into the cold night air. "So, what next?" Theo inquired of Bernard.

"I would invite you over, but I think you should be with Jules."

Theo nodded reluctantly. "I know. It's a delicate time. I wish I could be with you."

Bernard reached his arm around Theo and squeezed him tightly. "Thanks for the conversation. I'll see you tomorrow, then?"

"Can't wait," Theo replied. He leaned toward Bernard and gave him a chaste kiss on his cheek.

They walked in opposite directions, each glancing back at the other as they continued along the pavement. Bernard climbed the stairs to his apartment, opened the door, turned on some lights, and walked toward the fireplace. He lit a fire, poured a glass of wine, and sat in front of the flickering flames, staring meditatively. He realized that his life had forever changed, and as strange as it seemed, it felt oddly good.

10

Chapter Ten

Bernard rang the Decker's bell, and Zoe came running to the door. "Bernard, Bernard, *Sie sind hier!*"

"Zoe, how delightful to see you!" He handed her a little gift he had picked up earlier. She ripped it open, and a colorful scarf floated out of the packaging.

"Thank you! We missed you. Can you sleep over here tonight?"

Bernard looked up at Theo, who came toward the door, grinning. He put his hand on her head and said, "We'll see, Zoe. Can you take Bernard's coat? I'll bring him into the living room."

Bernard walked in behind Theo. Jules was sitting in a large chair by the fireplace with a glass of water in her hand. She smiled, stood up, and gave Bernard a warm kiss on both cheeks. "I'm so glad you're here."

"My pleasure," is all he managed to get out.

Theo handed him a glass of wine, and they sat together around a small table of appetizers. There was a strained silence before Jules started. "Sorry to drag you into all of this, Bernard."

"Hmm, not a problem," he replied. Her comment made him realize he had stepped into a complicated domestic nightmare, certainly not something he had ever anticipated.

They discussed pleasantries — the weather, skiing, politics — and then gathered at the dinner table. Dinner was strained, a heavy unspoken agenda looming overhead. Jules had made a savory salad and some poached salmon. She was pleasant, but not her usual effusive self. She avoided Bernard's glances, fussing over Zoe and the food. Theo seemed on alert, fearing he might make a misstatement or touch a raw nerve. Bernard decided the best strategy was to drink heavily, replenishing his glass often. Even Zoe sensed the tension. Her legs were still, her smile muted, and her appetite diminished as she pushed food around the plate.

After dinner, Zoe went to her room and Jules, Theo, and Bernard gathered in the living room in front of the fire.

Jules took the lead. "So, Theo told you about the pregnancy."

"Yes. Congratulations."

"Hmm," she murmured, then continued, "Well, it was a bit of a surprise."

Theo sat quietly to the side, watching Bernard listen attentively to Jules.

"This is all complicated, and I'm not sure how to formulate my thoughts," she began and then paused. Continuing, she said, "I've given this some thought. I'd like you and Theo to raise the baby."

"Yes, Theo mentioned that. Explain to me why." Bernard sat nervously on the edge of his chair, his arms crossed over his knees.

"I know. It seems out of the ordinary, but there is some logic to it."

Bernard nodded for her to keep going.

"I know we are way ahead of ourselves here, and we have time. Theo and I are very fond of you. Zoe has taken to you right away and, well, Theo hasn't been happier." She looked over at Theo.

"But what about you?" Bernard replied warmly.

"I've told you where I'm coming from. I'm sort of relieved and need to step back without stepping away from my family, which means everything to me."

"But don't you have needs?" Bernard insisted. He continued to find Jules very sensual, erotic, provocative. He couldn't imagine her not wanting to connect physically with someone.

"Our sexuality, or eros, isn't always about sex. It is also about affection, personal connection, and intimacy. Because of my trauma, sex isn't satisfying. In fact, it's frightening and brings up terrible memories. I love touch, warmth, beauty. I love friendship and the intimacy that trusting friends can share."

"Assuming Theo and I get along," he looked over at Theo, who smiled, "what kind of situation is that going to put you in if we are raising your baby – that is yours and Theo's baby?"

"It's very unconventional, I admit. But families today are increasingly different. There are single-parent families, traditional heterosexual families, and gay families with adopted kids or kids conceived through IVF and surrogacy. There are multigenerational families and divorced and blended families. In fact, most kids today do not grow up in the so-called traditional intact heterosexual family – something that may not have been so traditional after all. I want to be part of a movement to support diversity. I want Zoe to grow up in an environment where gender isn't linked to traditional roles. I want her to see two men raising a child, her brother or sister. I want her to know that there are different ways to love and different relationships that support a person's path, whatever that might be."

"Wow!" is all Bernard could say. "I'm impressed," he added.

Theo looked over at Bernard, concerned about his reaction, and then Bernard asked, "How does this all work practically in terms of living arrangements?"

"We'll have to figure that out."

"Any ideas?" Bernard inquired, "And, by the way, remember I live in Boston."

"Hmm, yes, that is a bit of an issue," Jules agreed.

"And," jokingly he added, "I'm not sure things will work out with Theo. We don't know how he handles domestic chores."

"Oh, that is a problem," she said emphatically. "But maybe we can train him."

Theo interjected, "Hey!"

"All joking aside, I've watched you two and have a good feeling about the future. You're both very thoughtful, sensitive, and compatible. I love the way Zoe has warmed up to you, Bernard, and how you bring out the best in her. I also like how you make me feel."

That was a surprise, Bernard thought to himself. He smiled.

"There are lots of options. There's a unit for sale next to ours in Bern. We could have adjacent apartments where Zoe and her brother or sister can play and spend time in both places. We could do something similar here or use this as a place for us to spend time together."

"And Boston?"

"Well, we might have to reconsider that," Jules noted. "I have some ideas."

Bernard wasn't entirely upset about the idea of moving to Switzerland. There was little holding him in Boston – no parents, wife, job – and his daughter was estranged from him.

"What do you think, Bernard?" Theo asked thoughtfully.

"It's a lot to process."

"Take your time," Jules interjected. "It's new to Theo and me as well. We'll all have to sort through this."

Bernard then turned to Theo. "What do you think? You haven't said much."

"I'm as surprised as you, although I'm not surprised by Jules' ideas. She's always been imaginative, thinking outside of the box. I like that about her."

"What about your job? I can't imagine Swiss government agencies will take warmly to a family like this," Bernard observed.

"Jules and I discussed that. I have a lot of seniority, and it would be difficult for them to remove me without exposing bias. But we would have to be careful. Jules and I would probably have to remain married, and the baby would be officially ours."

Bernard considered the implications of what Theo had just shared and realized he would have little legal or official standing – not married, not the adopting father of the baby, and perhaps not even possessing a residency visa to remain in the country. This sounded more and more like being a fifth wheel than a spouse or companion. It was unsettling.

Jules noticed Bernard's reticence and reached over to him, "Bernard, Theo is omitting to tell you that we discussed drafting a will or testament that would outline the relationships we have so that even if legally we fell under traditional categories, on paper and before a witness, we would make promises and vows that align with our new status."

Bernard wasn't entirely sure that would resolve future complications or put his own mind at ease in terms of his status with Theo and with Jules.

Theo then added, "Bernard, it's understandable that you would feel vulnerable in all of this. I can only hope that with time, we will all feel secure with each other and trust the commitment and support we are promising. It will be something we have to remind each other of frequently and find ways to celebrate and mark what we have."

Bernard leaned back in his chair, took a long sip of wine, and pondered what was being proposed to him. It felt bizarre yet appealing at the same time. He wondered if there might be a way to use the arrangement to his advantage – a way to foil Angela and Susan in some way.

"Bernard! Bernard! Are you still there?" Theo inquired as he noticed Bernard staring off into space.

"Oh yes, I just got lost in my thoughts. Sorry."

"You had quite a smile going on. What was so funny?" Jules asked.

"Oh nothing," he said evasively.

"*Et alors?*" Theo added, piercing the heaviness in the room and offering an opportunity to move onto something lighter.

"Well, gentlemen, if you will excuse me, I need to get some much-needed rest," Jules said as she stood up, dropped the glass off in the kitchen, and walked down the hall to the main bedroom.

Bernard gave Theo an inquisitive look. Theo began quietly, "I made up the guest room for us. It's official. We're having a sleepover. Be careful, though. Zoe is likely to join us early in the morning."

Bernard raised his eyebrows. "Unbelievable!"

They tip toed down the hall, past Zoe's room, and closed the door to the guest suite. Bernard looked for a lock. There was none. He looked for a chair to prop against the door, and Theo looked askance at him. "There's no need. We'll be fine."

Bernard wasn't sure he could relax when Jules or Zoe could bounce in at any moment. Theo led him to the bathroom and opened the cabinet. "These are for you," pointing to a toothbrush, razor, and a variety of toiletries. Theo guided him back into the bedroom and opened the armoire where Theo had hung some pants, a sweater, and, in the drawer, underwear and socks. "I hope I got the right sizes."

"When did you do all of this?"

"This afternoon."

"You don't waste time."

"I've been waiting for this a long time. I've rehearsed it over and over – although never with Jules and a new baby in the picture."

Bernard reached over and gave Theo a kiss. Theo took hold of Bernard's face and kissed him back. "I'm so happy."

"Me, too, although you're still on probation.

Theo faked a pout and said, "Let's get you ready for bed."

"Theo, just a minute. Let's sit." They sat down on the edge of the bed. Bernard continued, "This is all very new to me, and it seems like it is moving fast and unconventionally. Just know that I'm not very relaxed yet. Take it slow with me."

Theo wasn't sure what Bernard was referring to – whether it was about sex or about the arrangement, or perhaps about everything. "I will. Don't be afraid to talk to me and let me know what you're feeling."

Bernard nodded.

Theo then reached down, unbuckled Bernard's pants, pulled the zipper down, and slipped his hand in slightly over the edge of his undershorts. "What are you doing?" Bernard interjected. "I thought we were taking it slow?"

"I'm getting you ready for bed."

Bernard felt himself become aroused, a hard protrusion pushing up through the open zipper. Theo kneeled down and removed Bernard's shoes and socks, and he pulled down his pants. He stroked Bernard's thighs and rubbed his hands along the back of his calves, playing with the dark hair that covered his olive skin. He squeezed in between Bernard's legs and began to tug the waistband of his shorts with his teeth. He could feel Bernard tremble but, as he looked up, he could tell it was pleasure, not nervousness.

Bernard reached for Theo's arms, felt the firmness of his biceps, and pushed against them. Theo stood up, his crotch in Bernard's face. Bernard reached for the zipper and pulled it down. He unbuckled the belt and let Theo's trousers fall to the floor. He, too, was aroused.

Bernard reached behind Theo and held his buttocks, pulled him toward him and kissed his shorts, feeling the hardness underneath. He breathed in the sweet mustiness emanating from the dark blue cotton fabric and dug his face deep into the folds. He massaged the upper back of Theo's legs, pressing him further against his face. He slid his hand up under the shorts and felt the warm, soft skin.

Bernard stood, raised his arms, and let Theo lift off his sweater. Theo ran his hands over Bernard's chest, playing with the soft, dark hair that circled his pecs and ran down his slim abdomen. He let his hand teasingly graze the hardness at the top of Bernard's shorts.

Bernard slid his hands up under Theo's shirt and squeezed his pecs that were hardening with arousal. Theo opened his mouth, and Bernard responded with a deep kiss. His heart raced, thinking about the forceful strength of a man devouring him. He had never felt such passion, all his inhibitions melting away.

Theo reached behind Bernard, and with his large hands, squeezed each buttock firmly. He ran his fingers deeper and deeper between them as Bernard moaned. Theo then lowered his hands and, with a firm, locking grip, lifted Bernard off his feet and tossed him onto the bed.

Bernard looked up at Theo's ravenous face. Theo began to kiss Bernard's neck and collar. He then swiveled so that he faced the foot of the bed and licked around the edges of Bernard's shorts, slipping his fingers inside the leg openings to feel Bernard. Bernard sighed and found himself tugging at Theo's shorts.

Theo swiveled back and opened his mouth over Bernard's, kissing him deeply. Bernard reciprocated while massaging Theo's back and slipping off his shorts. Bernard wiggled out of his, and they both felt the raw, firm, hot touch of each other.

Theo longed to slide himself into Bernard, but held back, respecting the novelty of it all. He lifted Bernard's legs over his shoulders and pressed himself hard against Bernard, bending over to suck him.

Bernard groaned and pulled Theo up onto his chest, stroking him as he did, Theo arching his back in delight.

Theo rolled over onto his side, and Bernard continued to stroke him, occasionally sliding his hand in between his legs, feeling the moist contour of his thighs. Theo moaned and reached for Bernard. Although he was of smaller stature, he didn't lack for endowment. Theo smiled as he felt the long, hard firmness in his hands. He opened his mouth wide for Bernard's lips, each breathing each other in as they increased the movement of their hands.

Theo climbed back on top of Bernard, feeling the solidity, heat, and strained tension of their bodies pressed against each other. He moved himself up and down, remaining as close to Bernard as he could, feeling the softness of his foreskin.

Bernard felt Theo come on top of him, warm wet shudders pushing against his own erection. Then he felt an intense sensation rise within himself, exploding in tremors of pleasure.

They moaned in joy, laying peacefully in each other's arms. Neither was in a hurry to get up. Bernard rested his head on Theo's chest, feeling it rise and fall as he breathed. Then he said quietly, "Let me go get a towel," and slipped off the bed and wandered into the bathroom. He returned, dried them both, and then jumped back in, pulling the covers tightly around them and wrapping his arms snuggly over Bernard's shoulder. "I love you," he said to Bernard.

"I love you, too."

They both lay quietly for a few moments, contemplating the terrain they had crossed, and slowly, gradually, fell to sleep.

At 7, Zoe knocked on the door. Theo jumped up, reached over the edge of the bed for their shorts, put his on and threw Bernard's over to him.

"Come in, Zoe."

Beaming, Zoe walked into the room in her pajamas and jumped onto the bed where Theo and Bernard held the covers up to their faces. She gave them both a kiss, and then Theo pulled her over to his side and invited her into bed with him. "Mommy wants to know if you want pancakes for breakfast."

"Tell her that would be wonderful. We'll be out in a minute."

Zoe leaped out of bed and ran into the kitchen. Theo reached over and gave Bernard a kiss. Bernard, embarrassed, gave him a half-hearted kiss back and dashed to the bathroom to wash up. He pulled on a pair of jeans hanging in the armoire and looked for a sweatshirt in the drawer.

Theo used the bathroom and put on a pair of sweatpants and a stretch undershirt that showed off his physique. Watching him, Bernard felt himself get aroused again and walked over to the window to open the curtains and look at the snowscape outside.

Theo was already in the kitchen pouring coffee when Bernard followed. Jules gave Theo a kiss and Bernard an affectionate hug. "Pancakes good for you guys?" she asked, as if nothing out of the ordinary had taken place.

Bernard loved Theo's morning tousled hair and the casual elegance with which he leaned against the counter. Jules looked beautiful. Even without makeup, her darker skin radiating warmth.

Zoe was already at her seat, drinking milk, and pouring syrup on the first stack.

"Looks like a nice day to ski," Jules began. "Are you guys going out today?"

"Aren't you?" Bernard inquired.

"No, I thought I would take it easy. Zoe and I have some shopping to do."

Bernard looked at Theo, who looked at Jules.

Jules asked, "Whaaat?"

Theo winked at her. She winked back. "It will do you good," she added. "You'll need some carbs. I have a feeling you will ski hard today. It's cold."

"How cold?" Theo inquired.

"They say it's below zero and not expected to warm up."

"Hm," Theo responded. "How are you with ice, Bernard?"

"You're talking to a veteran New England skier. I can handle it."

They finished their breakfast, took showers, and dressed. They walked to Bernard's apartment, where he changed into ski clothes and grabbed his skis.

They walked to the First gondola, where a line had already formed. They climbed the steps, passed through the electronic ticket reader, and continued the clumsy walk forward. It was cold, and clouds of vapor puffed out of the mouths of skiers. They were wedged between two larger parties and ended up in their own gondola. The doors closed, the car rolled out of the station and then, catching the cable, rose quietly over the landscape below.

Bernard glanced out of the window as wooden chalets passed underneath, eventually giving way to a grove of pine trees covered in a frosty sheen, glistening in the morning sun. He looked at Theo, who was adjusting the goggles on his helmet. Bernard pushed his knee up against Theo's legs. Theo's dark ski pants stretched around his muscular thighs and were loosely open at his boots. Both had their jackets zipped up over their necks, wrapped in colorful gaiters, ready to pull up over their faces.

Theo looked up and smiled. There was an unspoken contentment that filled the space. Neither wanted to disturb it. Bernard looked out the window again, one of the ski slopes coming into view below them.

"The conditions don't look bad," Theo observed. A soft corduroy surface on the snow was still undisturbed at that early hour. Then they heard the harsh scraping sound of a few skiers making turns on the steep slope, evidence of an icy undersurface. "Maybe they're not as good as they look," he added after hearing the skiers below.

"We'll just take it easy. No need to tackle the entire mountain. Maybe some of the gentler slopes are less slick."

Theo nodded. "By the way, I like your new jacket. I had been eyeing something similar earlier in the season. Did you get it at Grindelsport?"

"Yes, as a matter of fact."

"Did Bruno help you?"

Bernard blushed. "Yes, why?"

"He's cute. Straight as they come, but cute."

Bernard laughed. He was unaccustomed to making observations about men, but realized he had an intuitive sensibility that Theo could put into words.

"What about Marc, Felippe's brother? By happenstance, I rode up the gondola with him my first week. He seemed to have had the eye for one of his male companions."

"Yes, he's the quiet type, cruising behind a mask of indifference."

"Precisely!"

Their cabin came up to the Bort station. The doors opened inside the station. They were riding further up, so they remained in place. A young man looked in, and Theo waved for him to join them. The man placed his skis on the rack and jumped in, taking a seat next to Bernard, facing up the mountain.

They said hello, and the man began to check messages on his phone. He was young, about thirty. He let his legs spread casually apart and rested his gloves on his right leg and part of his crotch. He wore race pants and was already sweating from early morning runs. Bernard caught Theo glancing over at him.

They continued the ascent and unloaded at the top, grabbing their skis and heading out onto the sunny but cold ridge overlooking the slopes below. The racer tossed his skis down next to Bernard and adjusted his goggles and gloves. He glanced over, and Bernard looked back. The racer then asked, "Do you know how to get to the Howald lift?"

Bernard responded, "I think you take that run over there and then keep hanging left. There's a terrain park. You can ski down it or on the other side."

"Thanks. You guys have a good day." He looked at both Theo and Bernard. Theo nodded. The man skied off.

"Well, he was definitely into you," Theo commented dramatically.

"I don't know what you mean," Bernard responded, his eyebrow raised.

"I'm going to have to keep my eye on you. You'll be eaten alive around here."

Bernard felt embarrassed. "I'm a middle-aged man."

"You underestimate your allure."

"I just don't get it."

Theo realized Bernard was naïve and wouldn't even know when he was being hit on. "That racer, he was hitting on you. He knew where the Howald lift was – he's from town – he just needed a line to open up a conversation."

"But I saw you looking at him earlier on the gondola. What's that all about?"

"I was staring him down. He had provocatively laid his gloves on his crotch, where there was little left for the imagination under his stretch pants. He kept glancing over at you, pretending to check his phone."

"But I would have thought he would have been into someone like you. You are breathtaking – tall and muscular – with these teddy bear eyes and dark blond hair that soften what would be an otherwise formidable presence."

"You noticed?"

"Of course, I did. From the first day."

Theo smiled and added, "A lot of people are afraid of me. You are approachable. You have a mystique to you. I was drawn to your English features – a soft gentle frame that is complemented by your grandmother's Italian influence – your darker complexion and hair. You're so sexy!"

No one had ever told Bernard he was sexy, and he tipped over on his skis. Theo reached to hold him up. "Maybe we should ski some," Bernard suggested self-consciously.

"Race you to the Shilt lift?"

"You're on," Bernard replied as he pushed off the ridge and down the slope.

They skied for a few hours and then took a break in the restaurant at the terminus station of the gondola. As they were seated, an attractive south American waiter approached and smiled warmly. Bernard was surprised, expecting a Swiss person instead. He was feeling good and greeted him, "*Hola.*"

The waiter looked surprised, and replied, "*Hola, que tal?*"

"*Bien. Quisieramos una jarra de vino – tinto – un litro.*"

"*En seguida.*" He walked back over to the bar.

Theo looked askance at Bernard, who shrugged his shoulders, "What?"

"You know what. I think I've unleashed a monster."

The waiter returned, placed glasses on the table, and poured the wine. Bernard looked up at him, but the waiter was looking over at Theo, who rested his chin on the back of his hand, staring.

As the waiter walked away, Theo rubbed his hand over Bernard's leg. "*Oye* – listen"

"I know what '*oye*' means."

Theo continued. "This is all fun and cute to be making eyes and comments here and there, but I want to make something perfectly clear."

Bernard gulped.

"You are the one for me – there are no others."

Chapter Eleven

Bernard exited the plane and made his way to customs, processing his passport and expedited entry papers at the kiosk and continuing to the first agent, who reviewed his documents. He expected special scrutiny but got none. He raised his eyebrows as the agent told him, "Welcome home!"

Bernard retrieved his suitcase and walked outside of the terminal into the chilly March air to look for a taxi. The line was thankfully short, and in a few minutes, he was riding past the skyline of Boston on the Mass Turnpike toward his home in Newton.

As they exited the highway and made their way through residential streets, Bernard noticed snow still lingering on the lawns from earlier storms. The taxi pulled up to Bernard's house. He paid the fare and rolled his suitcase along the sidewalk that had been cleared of ice in preparation for real estate showings.

Once inside, he turned on the lights and made his way into the living area. He surveyed the space, one that had been home for so many years but now felt ironically foreign. Everything was in place, as if time had stood still. He walked into the kitchen, the counter carefully staged with an espresso maker and a canister with utensils. His agent had decorated the dining table with a runner and a vase full of flowers. In the living room, someone had placed decorate pillows on the sofa and knick-knacks on side tables. Everything looked warm, contemporary, and ready to move-in.

Passing Angela's empty room, he walked into the main bedroom. He turned on a bedside lamp and approached the walk-in closet where half of the space had been emptied when Susan left the summer before. In his mind, he immediately began to identify things he would bring to Switzerland, articles he would donate, and stuff he would throw out. He was eager to move forward.

The house was cold, and he walked up to the thermostat to adjust the temperature. He heard the furnace kick on and the radiators rattle as the hot steam circulated through the house. He sat at his desk, pulled out his laptop, and typed an email to Theo. "I arrived safely. No problems at customs. At home now, sorting through things. I can't wait to return to Bern. Love, Bernard."

There was mail on the desk, and Bernard opened pieces that looked important. He had been banking and paying bills remotely, but there was some correspondence from the university about his pension and papers from the car company about his lease. He set them aside, went over to his suitcase, unpacked, took a shower, and went to bed.

The next morning, Bernard sat at the small kitchen table near a sunny window, checking emails and texts and enjoying a warm cup of coffee. The snow was melting, and patches of green grass and stone terraces revealed the contours of the gardens he had spent so much time tending over the years. A text appeared from Theo: "Got your email. Glad you are there safely. I hope things go well. Can't wait for you to come back, too."

Bernard's agent texted: "We have a second showing for a couple that is very interested in the house. Can you find something else to do around 1 PM?"

He texted back, "Good news. Yes. I'll be out of your way."

Bernard spent the morning filling boxes with things he would donate to charity. By the end of the morning, he had four large boxes of books, clothes, pots, and pans. He put them in his car and headed into the city to leave them at a charity, have lunch, and then meet with human resources at Generix.

Jules had used her connections to get Bernard a job at the company. His language skills and residency in Boston were perfect, and his experience at the university fit the department's need for someone who was comfortable working with an internationally diverse workforce. He had met with the team in Basel, but he was eager to connect with upper management in Cambridge.

He entered the modern building in Kenmore Square, where a security guard took him to a set of offices on the eighth floor with magnificent views of Boston. A few minutes later, a young man, about 30, greeted him, "Mr. Williams. Welcome!"

"The pleasure's all mine," he said as he shook his new boss's hand.

"Your trip from Switzerland went well?"

"Yes. No problems."

"Come into my office here. I know we spoke via video conference last week, but it would be nice to get to know you a little better in person."

Bernard nodded.

"I understand you are from the Boston area, but now live in Switzerland."

"Well, that's all being worked out. I'm in the process of selling my home in Newton and applying for residency status in Switzerland."

"As you know, that is perfect for what we have in mind. We want someone who can travel back and forth between Switzerland and the US without problems and manage a diverse workforce.

Your language skills and extensive travel background come highly recommended."

"Thank you. I look forward to the work."

Bernard gazed at the handsome young man sitting across from him. He found out that his supervisor was an MIT graduate, was managing the HR department of a successful international pharmaceutical company and lived with his male partner in the Seaport district of the city. He marveled at how the local workforce had changed over the years.

He could not disclose his own orientation to him for the moment, as it was part of a carefully veiled arrangement with Theo and Jules. Theo and Jules remained married. This protected Theo's job and the status of their future son. Bernard was "their friend" from the States who landed a lucrative job at Generix.

"I understand you are selling your home in Newton," the young man continued. "Are you going to get a place in the city?"

"For the time being, I think I will just stay at hotels when I come here for meetings. I'm looking for a place in Bern now."

"Well, if you ever need an agent here in Boston, I have some friends who can help you find a place."

"Thanks," Bernard said warmly.

The two of them discussed the responsibilities of the work, the logistics of communication and office space in Basel, and then exchanged pleasantries about Boston and its development as an educational and pharmaceutical hub. Bernard left Generix headquarters and made his way back to Newton when he got a text from his agent. "Full offer, contingent on inspection. They are ready to move in as soon as possible."

Bernard texted back, "Great news!"

Back at home, Bernard texted his daughter. "Hey honey. I'm in Boston. Would you like to get together for dinner?"

"I have some previous engagements here in Providence. I'll have to pass this time. Maybe next time you're in town," she texted back.

Angela had continued to be hostile and cold. She returned to Boston from her ski trip and told Susan about Bernard's coming out – which didn't surprise her. As predicted, Susan used the information to deflect attention from the real reason she had divorced him. Bernard felt marginalized but relished the idea that a whole new adventure had opened for him and that he felt loved like never before.

His phone vibrated, and he picked up the call from his agent. "Bernard, I have a contract for you to review and sign if it looks good. The couple wanting to buy your home are paying cash. How quickly could you move?"

"Do they want any of the furniture? I could be out in a week or two."

"Funny you should ask. They were wondering what you might charge for it. They like your taste, and it would help them move things along. They're moving from New York. Their jobs have already begun, so the sooner they can get settled, the better."

"Let's make them a good offer on the furniture. It would save me time and money having to get rid of it."

"I'll be back in touch with you soon."

"Thanks so much for your work."

Bernard hung up and sat down at the kitchen table, pouring himself another cup of coffee. "Wow!" he said to himself, "This is all working out quickly!"

Bernard was dying to tell someone everything that had transpired over the past couple of months. He lamented the estrangement from his daughter, but realized it made it easier to preserve some of the more confidential aspects of the arrangement. Most of his and Susan's friends had taken her side, and he certainly didn't want to get into the information he had found out about her, anyway. There was one colleague at a university in New York that he felt like he could confide in. He looked up his contact information.

Martin recruited foreign students, too. They had been classmates at Yale, Martin having grown up in Philadelphia. Martin had come out to Bernard during their sophomore year, a not-so-subtle attempt to make a pass at Bernard, who, out of touch with his own sexuality, simply offered support. Over the years, they had remained friends. Bernard had heard about all the comings and goings of Martin's boyfriends. He had a terrible record of coupling with cute but unfaithful men.

He texted Martin, "Martin. How are you? I'm in Boston and wondered if you are in New York and might like a visit."

Martin texted back, "I'm in between trips. You're welcome to crash at my place if you like. It would be great to see you."

Bernard hesitated, then replied, "That would be nice if not too much of a bother."

"When might you come?"

"This weekend?"

"Perfect. I don't have plans. Why don't I get some tickets for a play?"

"Sounds good. I'll take the train tomorrow afternoon and a taxi to your place."

"Looking forward to catching up," Martin texted back.

The next afternoon Bernard boarded the train in Boston and began his trip to New York. The scenery in Rhode Island and Connecticut was beautiful. Patches of snow in the woods were melting, and the colors of the sea were changing from grays to blues. The ride from New Haven to Manhattan reminded him of his undergraduate days and the frequent trips into the city he used to make. As the train approached Manhattan, the majestic skyline came into view, and his heart raced in anticipation.

At the station, Bernard hopped into a cab for the West Village, where he found Martin's condo and rang the bell. Martin buzzed him up, and Bernard climbed the stairs to the fourth floor.

Martin stood at the open door with arms outstretched for Bernard. "Oh, my God! It's been too long," he said as he gave him a warm kiss on the cheek.

"You look good as usual," Bernard said, looking up and down Martin's lean, muscular torso.

"You look different," he replied, stepping back and giving Bernard a careful glance.

Bernard grinned. Martin looked suspicious. "You met someone, right?"

Bernard nodded.

"Well, come in. Let me take your coat, and you'll have to tell me all about her."

Martin took Bernard's coat and hung it on the hook near the door. He rolled in his suitcase, and they both walked into the large parlor area. Martin had bought the condo years ago when prices were reasonable. He had a large apartment with high ceilings and great access to transportation and parks. Bright orange flames danced in the gas fireplace, and a plate of cheese and crackers were set on the coffee table.

"What can I get you to drink?" Martin began.

"How about some red wine?" Bernard walked around the room as Martin went into the kitchen to pour the wine. "Looks like you have some new artwork."

"Yes, you know me. It's hard to go to Ptown without bringing something home."

"I like this one," he said, pointing to an impressionistic image of a wharf and boat as Martin came back into the room.

"Ah, yes. I got that for Frederick. He forgot to take it with him when he left in November.

"What is it with you and your boys?"

"I don't know. I seem to have a terrible history, right?"

"As long as you're happy and safe."

Martin nodded. "So, tell me. What's new? Weren't you in Switzerland?"

"Yes, I spent the last two months there."

"Wow. How was that?"

"Well . . ." Bernard glanced at Martin with a sheepish grin.

Martin leaned forward. "Spill!"

"As you guessed, I met someone."

Martin bounced up and down in his chair. "What's she like?"

"It's not a she – it's a he!"

Martin's mouth dropped. "Oh My God – you're pulling my leg!" He took a long dramatic sip of wine and leaned forward.

"Nope!" Bernard said, hiding his own grin behind his glass of wine.

"I always knew it. You were too cute and fastidious to be straight."

"I wish you had told me that a long time ago. It would have prevented a lot of unnecessary distress."

"Admit it. You've had a good life with Susan and Angela. Now you're ready for your new chapter."

"You're right. I feel like it is good timing."

"Tell me all about him."

"Well, it's complicated."

"Girl! I can call you that now, right? Girl, it's not love if it isn't complicated!"

"He's married."

"To a woman?"

Bernard nodded.

"And?"

"Well, he and his wife have known for a while that he's gay. She was sexually assaulted at work, and their relationship is a good cover for them, for their high-security jobs. She's encouraged him to get involved with me."

"That's very unconventional. I like it."

"There's more."

Martin looked alarmed.

"His name is Theo, hers is Jules. Jules is pregnant, and she wants Theo and I to raise it."

"Whaaat?"

"I know. A bit odd, right?"

"I'd say. But tell me more."

"Well, Theo works in government and Jules at a pharmaceutical company. Theo has to remain relatively closeted, so his and my relationship is secret. I'm their friend from the States."

"This looks like a catastrophe waiting to happen."

"I know. Isn't it exciting?"

"What's gotten into you? You've always been so conventional."

"Time for a change," he said with a smile.

"So, are you moving to Switzerland?"

"Yes. I have a job with a company based there and in Boston."

"And Angela?"

"She's angry at me now. She thinks I'm the cause of estrangement from Susan."

"And aren't you?"

Bernard hesitated. "Not really. She had an affair with a faculty member at another school and married him," Bernard said, concealing the real underlying reasons.

"So, tell me more about Theo. I love the name!"

"He's younger – 40. He's built like a Swiss farmer — tall, stout, muscular. He's got dirty blonde hair and a cute face – with angular jaws and a round nose and dimples."

"Pictures?"

Bernard pulled out his phone and scrolled through the

photographs, pulling up one with him and Theo on the slopes. He leaned over to Martin and enlarged the picture.

"Wow! He's handsome. I thought I might win you over, but I see I don't have a chance."

"Oh Martin, you're handsome as ever. If I hadn't fallen in love with Theo, you would have been first in line."

Martin pressed his lower lip into a pout and then smiled playfully at Bernard. "This calls for a celebration! I have tickets to a play, and we'll go to a fabulously gay restaurant afterwards!"

They finished their drinks. Bernard freshened up and slipped on a fresh pair of jeans, a new shirt, and the sweater he had bought in Bern. It was still cold, so he put on his heavy coat, a wool cap and scarf, and slipped on a warm insulated pair of boots. "All set?" he asked Martin, who was arranging his own scarf.

"*Andiamo*," Martin said excitedly. "Girls' night out!"

"I'm going to have to learn a whole new vocabulary," Bernard said, grabbing Martin's arm as they stepped out onto the sidewalk.

"I have a feeling it's your mother tongue, honey!"

They quickly hailed a cab and, in a few minutes, were at the theater. They took their seats and surveyed the crowd. "Either I was blind before or this looks like a much gayer crowd!"

"Honey, you were blind, but it is a gay crowd tonight. They're all coming out for Karen Olivo! She's been on a bit of a hiatus, and everyone is excited. Wait till you see her in this show!"

Martin leaned into Bernard's shoulder. Bernard enjoyed the touch and intimacy and felt like he was part of the tribe. It felt oddly comforting and familiar rather than strange. The man sitting next to him smiled warmly and asked, "Where did you get that sweater? It's very nice."

Bernard blushed and Martin overhead the exchange, leaning over to hear Bernard's response.

"In Bern – in a little boutique there."

"Oh. Yes. It has a European cut to it. Were you there for work?"

"Not exactly. I was skiing."

"Nice. Do you go often?"

"Not really."

Martin nudged Bernard and whispered, "Engage!"

Bernard began timidly, "Looking forward to seeing Karen Olivo?"

The young man beamed. "I can't wait. I've had these tickets forever! She's incredible!"

Bernard nodded, and Martin nudged again. "Are you from the city?"

"I live here now," the young man said. "By the way, my name is Jason."

"Bernard."

"Nice to meet you."

"So, you said you live here now? Where were you from?"

"Originally upstate."

"Where about?"

"Syracuse."

"Great city – with the university and all."

"Yes, but it's rather limited. I came here for work."

"What do you do?"

"I'm a lawyer."

Bernard felt another nudge from Martin. He feared his side would be bruised soon. The lights dimmed, Jason nodded to Bernard, who nodded back and then he leaned toward Martin, who whispered, "You're a natural."

"Well, I had a bit of prompting!"

Martin smiled. The curtain opened, and the play began.

After the show, Martin and Bernard went to a small restaurant nearby for dinner and, afterwards, Martin convinced Bernard to go with him to a gay club. "It's not a loud disco, it's quieter. They have jazz and a friendly crowd."

"Sounds like the place I went to in Zurich."

"You went to a gay bar in Zurich? It didn't take you long to spread your wings!"

"Long story, but it was an interesting experience. Met a cute guy."

Martin raised his eyebrows. "Before or after Theo?"

"In between!"

"Love it. You'll have to tell me more." They walked inside the club, checked their coats, and found a table against a side wall facing the stage. A man was playing piano and singing popular Broadway pieces. The venue was crowded with small groups of people standing, talking, and drinking. Martin surveyed the crowd, catching a few eyes here and there. Bernard nervously checked his phone for texts from Theo, not entirely sure if it was a good idea to come to a bar with Martin.

A middle-aged man approached them. As he got to the table he said, "Martin – what a pleasure to run into you here."

Martin gave the man kisses on both cheeks and then said, "Michael, I want you to meet Bernard. Bernard, Michael."

"A pleasure," they each said in unison.

"Can I offer you a drink?" Martin asked Michael.

Michael held up his glass of wine and said, "I'm good for now."

Michael was a tall African American with a muscular frame. He had a warm, affable, and gentle face – a prominent jaw, high cheekbones, and a large sexy nose. He had a short-trimmed beard that circled his mouth and lined his jaw and chin.

"Michael works at another university in human resources," Martin began. "Bernard used to recruit students like me in Boston."

"What are you doing now?" Michael inquired warmly.

"I just took a job with a pharmaceutical company."

"In Boston?" Michael inquired further.

"Yes," Bernard replied without elaboration.

"Bernard's being humble. He just landed a great job in human resources and will fly back and forth between Switzerland and Boston."

"Wow, that sounds exciting!" Michael said.

Martin looked over at Bernard, who detected a look of encouragement, as if Martin was trying to fix him up with Michael. Bernard shook his head imperceptibly to discourage him.

They turned toward the stage and listened to the music for a while. During the break, they continued to talk, Martin ordering another round of drinks. Bernard discovered that Michael knew his boss, Ryan, from a previous job, and spoke highly of him. Bernard then said, "I don't know how to put this, but if you are in touch with him in the future, can you keep my gay status discrete?"

"Sure, but why? Ryan is out."

"It's not Ryan I'm worried about. There are some complicating things in Switzerland."

"Ahh. I see. No problem!"

Martin looked inquisitively at Bernard, sensing there was more to the story than Bernard had even disclosed. He took another sip of wine but kept a close eye on Bernard as they continued to listen to the music and chat in between songs.

Around one o'clock, Martin and Bernard headed home. It had been a while since Bernard had partied so late. "How do you do it?" he inquired of Martin, who seemed ready to go to another club.

"Vitamins!"

"You'd have to pump me with a lot of vitamins to have me do this very often! I'm pooped!"

"How are you going to keep up with your young Swiss lover, my dear?"

Bernard thought back to their skiing and the challenges he lived up to on the slopes. "I can handle him well enough."

"I can't wait to meet him someday soon!"

"You will. Do you ski? You'll have to come over in the winter!"

"My skiing days are over, but I'll come to sit around the fire and drink coco!"

"I can see you now, sitting by the lodge fire and hitting on the ski instructors at the end of the day."

"Are you a mind reader, too? That was the exact vision that came to me!"

"Why am I not surprised?" Bernard said, leaning into Martin as they approached the front of his building and made their way inside.

The next day, after breakfast, Bernard took the fast train back to Boston to sign papers on the sale of his house. He spent the next couple of days emptying cabinets and drawers of things he no longer intended to keep. He packed things into boxes that he would send to Switzerland. Angela continued to make excuses for not meeting with him.

Theo texted pictures of an apartment in the same building and on the same floor as his and Jules's place and suggested they purchase it together. Bernard agreed and, after the sale of the house, wired money to Theo. Everything was moving at a swift pace.

At the end of the week, he was taking a taxi to Logan airport and walking up to the Swiss Air counter to check in. "Mr. Williams, I see you are in business class. We can accommodate the extra luggage you have," she said as she looked at the large pieces he had rolled up to the counter.

"Thanks. I didn't realize I had so much to pack."

The agent smiled. She handed him his passport and boarding pass, tied labels onto his luggage, and pointed him toward security. A few hours later, he was leaning back in his seat, having a drink, and watching the Boston skyline recede from view and the dark sky over the Atlantic beckoning a new beginning.

12

Chapter Twelve

Bernard walked out of the customs area, where Theo was waiting anxiously. He approached him and gave him an enthusiastic but measured embrace, and whispered in his ear, "I love you."

Theo beamed and nodded. "Sorry we have to be so discrete. Let's go. The car is in the garage."

"I can't believe this is home," Bernard said with a big smile, looking over at Theo.

"Yes, I'm sure that must seem strange."

They walked into the garage, paid for their parking ticket, and went to the car. Once inside, Theo rubbed Bernard's legs and leaned over to give him a warm kiss. Bernard rested his hands on Theo's leg and noticed he was getting aroused.

"I can't wait to get you home," Theo said with emotion.

They exited the car park and took a series of highways around Zurich towards Bern. The snow had melted at lower elevations, with vibrant green shoots of grass and spring crops emerging on the farmland outside the city.

"Any news on the apartment?" Bernard began.

"We're still working on it. There seem to be some title complications. It's a historic structure, so there were some discrepancies in the records."

"Too bad. Do I need to get a hotel room?"

"Are you kidding? Zoe will sleep with Jules, and you and I are in her room."

"But that's a hobbit bed!" Bernard protested.

"We got her a new big-girl bed. Not to worry. So, how was the closing in Boston?"

"No problems. All good."

"Did you see Angela?"

"No. She's still angry."

"She'll come around at some point."

"I hope you're right."

The ride to Bern was quick, and they exited the highway, weaving their way deeper into the middle of Bern. Traffic was heavy, and Bernard took the time to observe the details of his new home. People were still bundled up against the damp cold, and slushy piles of snow lined the sidewalks, as in Boston. Trams made their way along tracks in a reserved pedestrian area, and cars were restricted to one lane, evidence of the Swiss preference for public transportation. Shop windows were decorated with Easter eggs and chocolate. Clothing stores were already displaying summer attire. Bernard was eager to experience summer in Switzerland, hiking in the mountains, and swimming in the lakes.

Theo glanced over and asked, "When do you go to Basel for your first day? You and Jules could commute together."

"Hmm," Bernard mumbled, eager to preserve some boundaries. It was all feeling very enmeshed. "I begin in a week, although there are some things I'm already working on remotely."

Theo nodded. They turned down a residential street of apartment buildings, six story structures that had been built after the war. They had historic charm and were popular with career government employees. Most were faced with white plaster and had red tile steep-pitched roofs with dormer windows. There were small gardens in front of the buildings with larger ones in the back where, in the summer, residents gathered for barbeques and picnics. At the end of the block, there was a small grocer, a dry-cleaner, and a hardware store.

"Here we are. Let me find a parking place. Ah, there's one," he said, pointing to a space up the road. Theo parked, and they walked toward the apartment.

"Can we at least see the new place?"

"I'll see if I can get a key later."

Theo entered the code to get into the building, and they took the elevator to the fourth floor. Bernard was about to turn right toward Theo's apartment when Theo grabbed his arm and pulled him left.

"What?" Bernard protested.

Theo pulled out a set of keys, dangled them in front of Bernard, and plopped them in Bernard's hand. "Surprise!"

Bernard's brows arched up, and he chuckled. "Oh my God, you didn't?"

"It's all set. We have the only two units on this floor. It's perfect."

Bernard inserted the key and opened the heavy wooden door to a cozy foyer with hardwood floors, coat hooks, and a bench for changing shoes. The foyer opened to a large parlor with tall windows overlooking the tops of the adjacent residential buildings, a few steeples rising at the edge of the district, and a hazy view of snow-covered mountains in the distance. "Oh my God," Bernard said, walking toward the windows and the sunny view outside. "This is magnificent!"

Theo walked up behind him and reached his arms around his

chest, and gave him a warm hug, resting his neck on Bernard's shoulders. "So, you like?"

Bernard nodded, a tear streaking down his cheek. He turned around. "You already have furniture?"

"Well, these were some things that came with the place – a nice sofa, some carved wooden chairs, a nice Persian carpet, and a sideboard. We can change them if you want."

"No, they're actually quite nice. I like them."

"Let me show you the kitchen and dining area."

They walked to the right, where a dining table filled a small room with the same view of the city. Behind it was a compact kitchen with new appliances – refrigerator, stove, dishwasher – and a wall of white cabinets and a marble countertop. "I love this," Bernard said, as he ran his hand over the surface.

Theo beamed. He opened the cabinets where a set of plates, cups, and glasses were carefully arranged. "We have a few essentials to get us started. I thought we could go shopping later!"

"Nothing would make me happier," Bernard said. "Although a view of the bedroom might be a prelude to something more fun!"

Theo grabbed Bernard's hand and led him to the other side of the parlor into a suite with a bathroom next to the parlor and a large bedroom with views of the city as well. "I took the liberty of getting a bed for us. I hope you don't mind."

"I think I'll need to take it for a spin," Bernard said, pushing Theo down on top of the mattress. Theo didn't seem to resist, and they laid next to each other, staring into each other's eyes and rubbing their shoulders. "This is so magical!" Bernard whispered.

"It's surreal," Theo added. "I'm so happy. Thanks for agreeing to all this. I know it's a bit much."

Bernard leaned over and kissed Theo. He caressed the back of Theo's head, playing with his hair. Theo pulled Bernard up close to him, nuzzling his hardness against Bernard's abdomen. "You feel like home," Bernard said, unbuttoning Theo's top buttons and reaching inside his shirt to feel his warm, muscular chest.

"Do you want more of the tour?" Theo asked.

"Of what?" Bernard replied playfully.

"Whatever you'd like," Theo noted.

"I want to explore more of this, but show me the rest of the place first."

They got up. Theo opened a door to a large closet where he had already placed his clothes and a few that Bernard had left behind. "Wow, this is a nice size closet for a historic building."

"I think it was added, but it's certainly a large space. And over here is a utility closet with a washer/dryer and storage."

"Very nice. We won't have to go down the hall to do laundry."

"I have a feeling we'll be doing Jules's laundry instead!" Theo laughed.

"I like the furniture. Was it here or did you get it?"

"I picked out the bedroom furniture. I hope you like the bed – it's classic. And we don't need a dresser, but I got a nice armoire for decoration and extra storage."

"Is there a place for an office?" Bernard inquired, looking around.

"Let me show you."

They walked back into the parlor. Bernard hadn't noticed that behind the main living area was an alcove already filled with a desk and some bookcases. "The foyer divides a kitchen on one side and a small office on the other. It's a nice design."

"I love it. Although I could see sitting near the window over-looking the city and doing work. Could we get a little table to place here?" Bernard asked, pointing toward the tall windows facing out.

"I'm sure we can." Theo looked at his watch. "I think Jules and Zoe are waiting for us. They have lunch ready."

They walked out the door and down the hall, knocking on the

door. Zoe came to the door, opened it, and with a big smile, reached up to Bernard and said, "Uncle Bernard!"

"Zoe, I've missed you! You look radiant as ever!"

She grabbed his hand and dragged him into the apartment where Jules was standing. She reached over to Bernard and gave him a warm embrace and then kissed him on both cheeks. "*Bienvenue!*"

"*Merci. Je suis heureux d'etre chez nous!* – I'm happy to be home! How are you feeling?" he said, as he looked down at her tummy.

"I'm doing well, thanks. The morning sickness has passed."

"Glad to hear!"

Jules smiled warmly and said, "Come in. Zoe and I have made a little lunch for you guys. I imagine you are going shopping afterward, right?" She said as she looked at Theo.

Theo nodded.

Zoe led Bernard into the dining area, where salad, stew, and wine were ready on the table.

"So, your trip was good?" Jules inquired.

"No problems – not even at customs." He winked.

"Sounds like things went well with the sale of your house. So, everything has been moved. Chapter closed."

"Yes, it seems very strange. All I have is what I brought in my suitcases, a few boxes I shipped, and what I had left here. I'm looking forward to a new start. It's very surreal – a sense of being at home but not having entirely left Boston with the job and everything."

"It's a lot of change in a short amount of time," Jules added.

They ate their lunch, caught up on news, and Theo and Bernard excused themselves. They returned to their apartment to change and headed out to the shopping area to get things for the apartment. They went to a large department store and found essentials for the kitchen — pots, plates, bowls, and glassware. They would be delivered later that afternoon. They proceeded to a few men's clothing boutiques where Bernard bought jeans, sweaters, shirts, a casual jacket, and other essentials. They carted them back to the apartment before heading to the last stop, the grocery store.

"We need everything – flour, salt, pepper, other spices, sugar, butter, milk."

"And wine and coffee," Bernard underscored emphatically. Theo smiled.

In about an hour, their cart was full. They checked out and caught a taxi back to the apartment and began to place things in the cabinets. The doorbell rang an hour later with their kitchenware.

"I have an idea," Theo said, as they had collapsed on the sofa from exhaustion. "Let's go to the bistro nearby for dinner. Remember the one where we met a few months ago?"

"Yes. I would like to eat the food there - finally. If I recall, the last time we were there, I didn't eat anything."

"You drank like a fish, though."

"It was a rough day." Bernard noted.

"I'm sorry," Theo said, reaching across the table and brushing his hand.

"I'm glad you told me about Susan. It helped put things in perspective."

They put on their coats and walked out into the cold night air. They walked a few blocks to the bistro where the maître d' recognized Theo and showed them to a nice table. The restaurant was full. It was a classic French brasserie with tile floors, white tablecloths, dark furniture, and yellow antique globes hanging from the ceiling. Their server approached and handed them menus. He enumerated a few specials and took their drink orders.

"I can't believe you're here. What a gift!" Theo said warmly across the table.

Bernard smiled, blushed, and looked down at the menu. "What do you recommend?" he asked evasively.

"Well, last time I believe you ordered the *steak-frites*. You might try them this time."

"Ha ha!" he said in reply. "Sounds good, in fact."

The server returned with their drinks, and they ordered.

"So, Bernard Williams, we should get to know each other."

Bernard looked up at Theo, partly alarmed and partly amused. He realized they really didn't know each other that well, but were beginning a life together. What had possessed him to move so quickly – to sell his house and move to Switzerland to begin a life with another man – and his wife and child? "What do you want to know?" Bernard said.

"Everything!" Theo said enthusiastically.

Bernard looked off and formulated some initial thoughts. Who was he? How would he begin to describe himself - genes, geography, language, and family - or were those just the predispositions for what were more significant – the choices, decisions, and relationships that made up his life's narrative?

"I'm not sure I know how to begin," Bernard began timidly. "If we had met a year ago, and you asked me who I was, I would have talked about my job, my wife, and my daughter. I would have made reference to my parents and my ethnic heritage and perhaps enumerated a few pastimes, like skiing and gardening. But now I realize I am not a collection of nouns – son, husband, father, recruiter, skier, gardener – but perhaps a verb, an event, a happening."

"You're going philosophical on me now!" Theo said, contemplatively taking a sip of wine.

"I know. It's rather pretentious."

"No, continue. It's interesting."

"Well, so often we cling to the identities we create when there is so much more going on."

Theo nodded, as if to encourage Bernard to continue.

"I wasn't ready to come out when I was younger, and I married someone who was only superficially committed to our relationship. That set the stage for a new chapter and one that involved meeting you. You might not believe in destiny or synchronicity, but our being together could only have happened with an extremely unique set of circumstances aligning."

"So, you're saying that the last 20 years unfolded with this in mind?"

"I'm not so sure. That would mean there is a script written about our lives and we are just going through the motions – or perhaps another way of saying it – we are just actors playing a part in a story written by someone else," Bernard elaborated.

"I tend to think things are more random and accidental. Zoe's accident led to our meeting and so forth."

"Agreed. But Zoe's accident led to a not-yet-out gay man meeting a couple who were struggling with how to move forward in a way that honored their respective constitutions. That seems unlikely, or at least more meaningful than just coincidence."

Theo rubbed his chin pensively. The server brought them each a bowl of French onion soup, a savory steam rising from the charred cheese and bread covering the white ceramic bowls. Bernard grabbed his spoon and began puncturing the crusty top. "Hmm," he said as he took the first sip.

"Yes, they do a good job here," Theo noted as he dipped his spoon into his soup.

"So, what if from the vantage of our limited perspectives, things look accidental, but from a deeper level, we are more involved in constructing the plot?" Bernard proposed.

"What do you mean?"

"Well, is the self just our own ego identity or is there a part of ourselves that is more spiritual or metaphysical and has a more comprehensive perspective?"

"You lost me at metaphysical." Theo grinned playfully, but, in all seriousness, was lost.

"Jung – a Swiss psychologist – hypothesized that the self is connected to a more collective self or consciousness. He did all sorts of work in the paranormal and concluded that we are part of some interconnected spiritual realm. The boundaries between people and time and place are more artificial and constructed than we would like to imagine."

"So, that would mean at some level we were connected already, right?" Theo proposed.

"That's what he and others have suggested. So, when you ask, 'who are you?' it's not so simple."

"I did feel an instant connection to you – and so did Jules."

"That's it exactly. Some energetic or wavelike pattern in the universal consciousness brought us together to continue our work and evolution as souls."

"How do you know that we are intended for each other?" Theo pressed further.

"First, it is the chemistry – a perceptible sense of affinity for someone – that draws up toward each other. Physical attraction is more than just lust and desire. The body and our desires are a place where the deeper self and soul are able to work."

"Amazing," Theo said, his face lighting up with awareness. He finished the last of his soup and placed the spoon under the bowl on the saucer. Bernard did the same. The server came and took the bowls and said their steak-frites would arrive shortly.

"But, after chemistry, the proof seems to be in the meaningfulness of the encounter. There's something that matches or fits between two or more people – a sense of purpose and common narrative that suggests that the coming together is not just accidental or physical but has a purpose. The three of us – you, Jules and I – maybe even Zoe and her future brother – fit. There's a logic or meaningfulness to our relationship that defies the ordinary and suggests the possibility of an extraordinary leap."

"Leap of what?"

"Leap of transformation or growth – a way to evolve into richer and more mature persons."

"I feel that with you," Theo said warmly to Bernard.

"I know this is inviting me to enormous growth," Bernard agreed enthusiastically.

"This is all very fascinating," Theo began, as the server approached their table and placed their plates of *steak-frites* in front of them. Theo reached for a few crispy fries as the server walked away. "I was raised Catholic but have been turned off by the antics of the Church in recent years and by what seems like empty rituals and formalities, but nothing substantial. What you are describing to me seems so much more spiritual and inspiring."

Bernard reached for the steak knife and began cutting into the juicy meat. He took a bite and said, "Wow! This is good."

Theo nodded. "See what you missed last time?"

"I was in shock!"

"Yes, I believe you were. Sorry about that."

"Quit apologizing. It was life transforming in a good way – painful – but transforming!"

Theo poured more wine into their glasses and looked intensely at Bernard. "I love you!"

"Me, too," Bernard replied. He took another bite of the steak and continued, "Back to the Church – I had the same reaction. I grew up in the Church and loved it for the most part. But with the abuse scandals and the lack of movement towards affirming women and gay people, I felt like it was being disingenuous. I did some reading on Jung, on mysticism, and then took a course in Reiki, and I realized there was so much spirituality at our fingertips, but we were never taught to recognize it, participate in it."

"So, on a more mundane note," Theo said, "what about your work, your love for languages, travel, and foreign students?"

"Yes, that seems to be part of my identity and, until recently, I'm not sure I ever considered why I was drawn to it. I think I know better now."

Theo nodded for him to continue.

"I think languages represent the ability to cross borders, to connect worlds separated unnecessarily. Maybe it was an intuitive sense that there was another world within me that needed addressing. It felt like with other languages, I could leave the familiarity and comfort of my existence and embrace another world of meaning and expression. It's not so much that I didn't like my life, it's that I felt like it was enriched when open to other cultures and peoples."

"I like that, and I see that in you. You know, Europeans embraced multilingualism, particularly after the first and second world wars. It was a way of trying to overcome the divisions that were artificial and fostered hostility," Theo noted.

"I wish Americans were more like that. I think in my work with foreign students, I grew to appreciate their vulnerabilities and the sense of marginalization they often felt. But I was always inspired by their desire to push themselves and to take advantage of the educational opportunities they had. I also wonder if deep down I sensed that I was different – that I was gay – and that other languages and other worlds were an echo of my own sense of vulnerability, marginalization, and a desire to connect."

"You say that so beautifully," Theo said warmly. "Since I came to recognize my own orientation, I have felt that same sense of isolation and ostracism. In some sense, I enjoy being a white male in a prosperous country in a position of authority and privilege. But I also know that I am not like my colleagues. The sense of being different and on the margins has helped me work for social justice – for ways to protect those who are most at risk and in peril."

"I like that about you!" Bernard said warmly.

"I think we have a bright and meaningful future ahead of us!"

"I agree." Bernard said. "And strangely, I think what Jules is proposing is visionary. We need to do more to affirm and embrace diversity in our families; to help children feel good about the different families they grow up in. Their parents don't need to feel like they are failures. Diversity is a strength and enriches our communities."

"Enough philosophy," Theo interjected. "I want chocolate and sex!"

"I saw you eyeing the profiteroles as we walked in."

"You're observant, Bernard Williams."

"I noticed you, didn't I?"

They both chuckled. The server came and took their plates. Theo ordered a plate of profiteroles and two espressos. "We should stop and buy a bottle of brandy on the way home. A nice after dinner drink on the sofa overlooking the soft lights of Bern would be romantic."

Bernard nodded.

The profiteroles came and were quickly devoured. Two espressos followed, and shortly thereafter, they had paid their bill, walked to the local liquor store, purchased a few things, and were in the elevator going to their apartment. Theo unlocked the door. They walked into the apartment, and in the ambient glow of the city lights, Theo pulled Bernard toward him, kissed him deeply, held him tightly, and said, "Welcome home!"

13

Chapter Thirteen

Two Years and Seven Months Later

"Zoe, can you help put candles on the cake?" Jules shouted from the kitchen.

Zoe skipped into the room in a pair of shorts and a summer blouse. The sliding glass doors were open to the deck, where chairs and tables were set for a party. Balloons were tied to posts and presents stacked on the terrace wall. A soft cool breeze flowed down the granite peaks of the Bernese Oberland, refreshed by glaciers hanging tenaciously over the village of Grindelwald.

Zoe stabbed the cake with 2 small blue candles and ran her fingers over the bottom edge of the frosting, licking them clean.

Bernard was helping Oliver change into clean clothes. He brushed his dark hair and tied his tiny tennis shoes and followed him slowly out of the bedroom into the living area where Jules's parents gave him a warm hug. Oliver hugged them enthusiastically, showing them a new stuffed animal he was holding.

Theo was standing near a grill preparing it for the BBQ. Some neighbors were talking with him, glasses of white wine in hand.

Jules's parents walked up to Bernard and gave him a warm hug. "Congratulations!"

"What do you think?" he inquired, his hand on Oliver's shoulder. "He's growing up so fast."

"He's such a prince. We're so delighted to see Jules so happy. And Zoe, she's become so much more talkative and self-confident. Thank you for all you do. We're so happy you're part of our family."

"Thank you. It's been an interesting couple of years."

"No doubt, but it all seems to be working out."

Bernard wasn't sure his in-laws were totally on board, but they did the best they could to make sense of things and be supportive. "Do you have a pre-school for Oliver yet?"

"We have been in conversations with a few institutes in Bern, and one of them looks promising. They were the only one that didn't flinch when Jules, Theo, and I all showed up."

"Well, they shouldn't. You're all great parents."

Bernard grinned. He walked over to Hans, Theo's partner at work, the only one Theo welcomed at gatherings like this.

"Hey, Bernard! You have your skis sharpened for the season yet?"

"Isn't it a little early, Hans?" They exchanged a warm hug.

"This is a great gathering you all have put on for Oliver's birthday. Congratulations."

"Thanks. We're glad you're here."

"I wouldn't miss it. By the way, did you get the dossier I sent you?" Hans asked discreetly.

"Yes, and I booked a flight for Boston."

"This is a delicate operation, and you're the best for it," Hans said with a wink.

Bernard smiled nervously. He officially worked for Jules's firm as a public relations liaison, but secretly worked for Swiss intelligence.

Hans was his handler. As far as everyone knew, Jules and Theo were still a couple and were close friends with the American Jules hired for her firm. Bernard had a resident visa, along with his American passport.

The couple with whom Theo was talking were gesturing dramatically. The man laughed, held his head back, and then placed his hand on Theo's shoulder. Theo looked over at Bernard and winked. Bernard walked over. The man removed his hand and hugged Bernard warmly.

As they hugged, Bernard whispered into his ear, "If I see you touching Theo again, you'll be toast! *Capisce!*"

"*Capisco*," he said back. "I understand."

Bernard smiled at the man's wife, who took a long sip of wine and dragged her husband over to Jules and her parents.

Theo and Bernard surveyed the terrace. "Nice party. And the weather held up!"

"August is usually very nice."

"I can't wait for winter."

"It's' going to be a busy fall. We're both traveling. We need to get Oliver settled sooner than later."

"We will. Don't worry."

Oliver ran past them toward the balloons. Theo untied one and attached it to his wrist. He flapped his hand vigorously as the balloon bounced in the soft sunlight.

Jules set some ceramic platters on the table, one filled with tomatoes, mozzarella, and basil and the other a Mediterranean couscous salad with peppers, cucumbers, tomatoes, and mint. Theo stood by the smoking grill and flipped some burgers. "Dinner will be ready in a few minutes," she announced to the gathering.

Zoe grabbed Oliver's hand and led him to the highchair. Bernard plopped him in and set a plate of pasta in front of him. Theo glared. "Pasta again? He'll throw it everywhere."

"He's Italian."

"No, he's French and Swiss – a big difference. I don't know where he picked up all the Italian behavior."

Bernard gestured to Theo, "I'm watching you."

Everyone gathered at the table, shared the platters, and prepared their burgers. When the meal was over, Jules brought out the cake with 2 lit candles singing happy birthday to Oliver. He tenuously blew on the candles, and everyone clapped.

Later that evening, after Oliver and Zoe were in bed, Bernard, Theo, and Jules gathered on the terrace for a drink. The sun had set behind the mountains but still cast a diffused late summer evening light on the village. A few candles flickered in the gentle breeze.

Jules broke the silence. "Have you heard from Angela recently?"

Bernard took a sip of wine and replied, "Nothing more than a simple text here and there."

"Are you going to see her when you are in Boston?" Jules pressed further.

"Not sure. She's still angry."

"After more than two years?"

"Her mother continues to stoke animosity. Susan has her convinced that it was my fault that the marriage and family fell apart."

"It's too bad you can't explain what happened."

"It's for the best. She's pretty conservative, and it's better to just let her stew."

"You don't think Susan suspects that you work for the Swiss, do you?" Theo inquired.

"No, she's on to bigger and more important things. After I was let go from the university, the government never gave another thought to my being a person of interest."

"But could Susan expose us if she knew who I am?" Theo asked further.

"She doesn't care enough to find out – and neither does Angela.

To them, we are just a couple of men getting our rocks off. Case closed. They think I had a mid-life crisis, moved to Switzerland, got a job using my language skills and, on the side, cruise men on the slopes."

"That about sums it up!" Theo laughed.

"Hey Jules, are you okay?" Bernard looked over at her.

"I'm perfect, thanks. It was a great day, no?"

"But are you really okay?" he insisted again.

"I am. I have never regretted my decision. Oliver calls me mom – and calls you two papa and papi. Zoe still treats Theo and I as her parents, but she considers you her fairy godmother come to life! Besides, I would have eventually lost Theo and, instead, kept him and traded up with a second handsome partner." She winked at Bernard. He chuckled.

"Hans is the only one I worry about," Jules added, looking over at Theo.

"He's got his own skeletons to hide. I made sure of that," Theo added. "Besides, he's had a perfect track record the last couple of years with you running missions in Boston. He's not going to mess that up with an indiscrete comment."

They continued their conversations, hugged each other good night, and settled into a nice rest.

A couple of weeks later, Bernard was on a flight to Boston. He was nervous. The new assignment was challenging – not in terms of risk – but in terms of logistics. It required just the right set of things falling into place.

The pilot announced the approach to Boston. It was dark, but Bernard could make out the lights of the freeways and the coastline of the south shore where he had grown up. As much as Bern and Grindelwald had become home, there was something comforting about returning to New England. He loved the sea air, the local accent, the familiar landmarks, and the food. He longed to stroll down Newbury Street, brush shoulders with countless college students, and grab a beer at a local bar with the Red Sox playing on big TV screens. Boston was a unique place – high tech and blue collar, a college town that doubled as a financial center and headquarters for large venture capitalists.

There were times he regretted having sold his home, but Generix took good care of him, putting him up at the Copley Plaza and providing a generous per-diem when he traveled.

The plane wasn't full, and lines at immigration were short. He had access to expedited processing, but always got pulled over for extra questioning.

"Your passport, please," the agent stated stoically. He was Irish, one of the old guard of Boston. It was late, and he was undoubtedly looking forward to the end of his shift.

As the kiosk scanned Bernard's document, the agent's forehead creased as he saw information pop up on the screen.

"What kind of business are you in?"

"I work for Generix pharmaceuticals."

"Your position?"

"Public relations."

"You're American?"

"Yes."

"And you have a Swiss resident visa?"

"Yes."

"Where do you live?"

"Bern?"

"And the headquarters for Generix?"

"Basel and Boston."

"Hm. And where will you be staying here?"

"At the Copley Plaza."

"Do you have family here?"

"A daughter."

The agent raised his eyebrow. "And who is Susan Figueroa?"

"My ex."

The agent typed something into his computer and read the response. He looked up at Bernard. "You're free to go. Welcome home."

Bernard chuckled at how unfazed he was now by border control, accustomed to the extra scrutiny. He had memorized responses to the same litany of questions that resulted in the same outcome each time. Bernard retrieved his bags and hailed a taxi for the Back Bay. En route, he texted Theo to let him know he had arrived safely.

He checked into the classic hotel, once the site of the Museum of Fine Arts, where he was upgraded to a suite overlooking Copley Square with its beautiful Trinity Church and Boston Public Library. The Back Bay still served as the cultural center of the city, the location of the best hotels, restaurants, and shops.

Bernard was tired from the day-long flight, undressed quickly, ordered a light meal from room service, and checked messages. He scanned photos, pulling up a playful image of Theo and Oliver at the birthday party. Oliver had inherited the dark hair and complexion of Jules and the larger frame of Theo. He was already taller than kids of the same age in his pre-school and had charmed the teachers with his verbal skills. It was hard to believe he was a father again and, regardless of outwards appearances, a husband, too.

The next morning, Bernard dressed in a casual business outfit – dark slacks, a tailored dress shirt and jacket – but no tie. The workforce at Generix was young. No one wore ties – most dressed in jeans, shirts, and sporty sweaters. He was senior management, but the culture of the company catered to the new workforce. He lined up at a local café where he enjoyed a double espresso, croissant, and fruit. He hailed a taxi and headed to Kendall Square, the base for the company.

He met with the staff, reviewed new press releases, and checked emails. His job was relatively easy. The company appreciated someone with his language and administrative skills and the ability to travel easily between Boston and Switzerland. They gave him a lot of latitude, which gave him time for other duties.

That evening, he had obtained a pass to attend Charles Figueroa's presentation at MIT. He hoped Susan wouldn't be present. Intelligence reported that she was in Prague. The lecture was at a local biotech company's auditorium and featured a discussion of geopolitical policies and public health. He sat at the front of the auditorium and waited for the lecture to begin.

Afterwards, as Charles circulated amongst attendees on the floor, he approached him. Charles recognized him immediately.

"Bernard, I didn't know you were in Boston. What beings you to the seminar?"

"Generix is interested in supporting international collaboratives."

"Ah, well, yes, I can see that it might be of interest."

"How are you doing?"

Bernard detected Charles's annoyance and replied evasively, "I'm fine. How are Susan and Angela?"

Charles bristled but replied, "They're good. Angela is in her junior year at Brown. We saw her off last week."

"Do you have any photos?"

Charles pulled out his phone, pushed the security sensor, and scrolled to his album. Bernard reached casually into his pant pocket and retrieved his phone. He opened his photos and said, "Let me share with you an old photo I found of Susan. I'm sure she would love to see it."

He pressed an airdrop app, one tailored by Swiss Intelligence, that detected Charles's phone and took advantage of its open status. It downloaded the photo, which included a secret code onto Charles's phone. The Swiss and their European partners hoped to use it to track and record Susan, who they suspected was conducting business between some corrupt US Congress members and eastern European oligarchs. He felt a slight vibration, confirming the transfer.

"Here's a photo of Angela in Providence. Doesn't she look good? She's been doing so well lately."

Bernard felt the statement was a not-so-subtle dig that she was better off with him and Susan in Boston. Bernard's only consolation was that soon Susan would be exposed, and Angela would discover the truth about her parents' divorce. He only hoped Angela wouldn't be hard on herself. He was eager to reconcile with her.

His business complete, Bernard took a cab back to Copley Square. En route, he texted one of his favorite restaurants in the South End for a reservation. He went to his room to freshen up, change into something more casual, and drop off his briefcase.

He waved the electronic key over the lock on the door and pushed it open. He thought to himself, 'I don't remember leaving a light on in the sitting area.' He made his way down the short hall and turned the corner.

"Hey handsome," Theo said warmly.

"Oh, my God! You're here!" Bernard exclaimed as he saw Theo sitting on the sofa. "How did you manage this? Where's Oliver?"

"Calm down. He is with Jules. I took an early flight via London."

"And your work?"

"They gave me some time off. I think Hans had something to do with it."

Bernard sat down on the sofa next to Theo and gave him an enthusiastic hug and a protracted kiss.

"You feel so good," Theo said as he rubbed Bernard's thighs.

"Are you hungry? I was going to go out for dinner."

"I'm starved."

"Let's go. I have a reservation at a nearby place. One of my favorites."

The evening was mild, and they walked a few blocks to Tremont

Street. Bernard pushed open the door of a small bistro with no more than a dozen tables. The hostess greeted him warmly and showed him a small table by the front window. "Jean, this is Theo."

"So, this is the Theo I've heard so many good things about." She eyed him up and down and said, "Hmm, delicious!"

Theo blushed, and Bernard held his hand firmly. They sat down in the tight space and stared into each other's eyes. "I still can't believe you're here. What a treat!"

A young, handsome waiter came to the table, nodding familiarly to Bernard, "Welcome back," and took a protracted look at Theo, noticeably taken by his size and foreign aura. He dropped off menus, and Bernard ordered a bottle of wine.

"You must have been planning this all along."

"It was Jules's idea. She knew I always wanted to visit Boston during one of your trips. She spoke to Hans, who said this might be a good one. We booked the flight, and I arranged for some vacation. By the way, Jules spoke to HR at Generix, and you have some time off, too."

"Wow! So, what do you want to do?"

Theo reached over to Bernard and held both hands. "First, I want to do you."

Bernard blushed and looked around to make sure no one had heard Theo. Their waiter winked from behind the counter.

"Really. What would you like to do?"

"I've never seen much of Boston or the area. Show me your favorite places. Oh, and Sara says we should go to Ptown or Provincetown. I'm not sure what it's called."

"It's called both. I never thought about going there, but it's a great idea. It's a picturesque coastal community with a lot of history, culture, and art – and it's one of the largest gay communities and resorts in the world. I have only been there a few times as a boy – never since I came out. It would be fascinating to go there.

The weather is still good. Even the beaches and water should be wonderful."

"That's what Sara implied. Let's do it."

Two days later, they hoped aboard the high-speed ferry to Provincetown. Weaving its way through picturesque rocky islands in Boston harbor, it skipped across Cape Cod Bay where, after an hour into the trip, a narrow bright strip of beaches and dunes came into view. As they got closer, the Pilgrim monument loomed in the distance, a tall granite tower celebrating the Pilgrims' landing there in 1620. Along the coast, majestic dunes topped with sea grass formed a protective barrier to marshes and a large harbor. The ferry pulled into the busy port, where hundreds of tourists milled about in galleries and shops.

Bernard and Theo disembarked, rolling their suitcases down the dock and a few blocks farther to the apartment they had rented. "It's so charming," Theo noted. "And, so gay!" he added, as a muscular shirtless man rode by on a bicycle.

"Hmm, yes," Bernard agreed, his head following one. "Since the early part of the 20th century, it became a haven for playwrights, artists, and performers. It increasingly attracted a gay crowd. Many have now made this their home – at least in the summers when the weather is pleasant." He looked up at the number on the building in front of them and said, "This must be it."

They climbed steps to a second-floor apartment overlooking the harbor. Opening the front door, they were greeted by a large room with floor to ceiling windows looking out over the water. The room was bright and airy, and Theo beamed with pleasure.

"Let's get unpacked. I want to visit some of the galleries, and re-member, we have dinner reservations at a restaurant on the water," Bernard said.

Theo changed into a pair of shorts and a pullover shirt he had packed for the late summer warmth. The shorts showed off his muscular legs, and all Bernard could do was think about rubbing his hands up under the shorts. He felt himself get hard. He walked over to Theo and gave him a kiss, rubbing his hands up under his pullover.

Theo moaned, reached under Bernard's shirt, and rubbed his chest. He pushed him toward the bed and lifted the shirt off.

"I thought we were getting ready for dinner."

"I am," Theo grinned, unzipping Bernard's shorts, and pushing him onto the bed. He pulled the shorts down and began to play with his undershorts, Bernard visibly aroused. Theo pulled off his shirt, and Bernard reached up and unzipped his shorts.

"Hey handsome," Bernard said, tugging Theo's briefs, exposing his engorged cock.

Theo leaned down and kissed Bernard deeply, holding him tightly in his arms. They laid next to each other naked, all their perfections and imperfections exposed in the unfiltered light beaming off the water and into the apartment, where a salty sea breeze blew the cotton curtains at the edge of the windows. They made passionate love to each other and dozed off into a light sleep.

Bernard stirred and broke the peaceful silence, "I love this, I love you!"

"Hmm, me too," Theo added.

"We should get going. Dinner is in an hour and a half."

"Is it okay that I had dessert first?" Theo inquired.

Bernard looked askance and Theo continued, "I know. That's a bit corny."

"Well, I already had the main course," Bernard noted, running his finger down Theo's abdomen.

They both chuckled, rolled off the bed, and put their clothes back on. They freshened up a bit, Theo asking Bernard, "Do I look okay?"

"Of course you do. Although everyone will know."

"Know what?"

Bernard just stared at Theo, who finally got it. Theo put his arms around Bernard, and they headed down the stairs. "I love how free I am here to express my love."

"It's a unique place, that's for sure."

They walked a few blocks toward the restaurant. The town followed the contours of the large natural harbor formed by the hook of the Cape. There was one main road that ran the length of the village, lined with historic New England clapboard houses. Since all the shops, galleries, and restaurants were on the main street, it was filled with pedestrians and cyclists who passed in all directions, gazing at one another. Here and there, views of the harbor opened through spaces between buildings, a gentle sea breeze cooling the air.

They stood at a ridge overlooking the main wharf, with boats moored in the shallow water between Land's End and the town beach. "It's so charming," Theo noted. "I love the brightly painted wooden structures and the charming shops."

"It doesn't hurt that there is so much eye candy walking around," Bernard added, as his eyes followed a shirtless young man walking past them on the way to the sandy shore.

"It is almost overwhelming," Theo added.

"Almost?" Bernard asked with sarcasm.

"Well, I'm focused on one person!" he said, squeezing Bernard close to him, who smiled warmly back.

They continued walking toward the restaurant, looking into galleries here and there. "It seems like everywhere you turn, there's an art gallery. I've never seen anything like this," Theo observed.

"Yes, it's pretty unique. Maybe a few other places are like this – Santa Fe, parts of Manhattan, a few small towns in California – but this is amazing."

They walked into a small gallery, bright lights shining on

colorful seascapes. The contrast of blues, greens, and yellows was mesmerizing.

"I love this one," Bernard began, pointing to one of the paintings.

"What about this one?" Theo inquired, pointing to another by the same artist.

"They're both beautiful. What if we got one for Jules and one for us – a celebration of our love and new home?"

"Great idea," Theo affirmed. They told the gallery owner they wanted both – and gave him the shipping address in Bern. He looked amazed. "We don't get too many people from Switzerland."

"I'm from here, but Theo, my partner, is from Bern."

"Nice to meet you both. Welcome." The owner said in reply.

"When do you think they will get to Bern?"

"It usually takes a couple of weeks. It shouldn't be long."

"Perfect," Theo noted, "Jules will be ecstatic."

"Who's Jules?" the gallery owner inquired.

"She's . . . well, how would we describe her?" Bernard looked at Theo.

"Our wife, our companion, our friend," Theo said.

The gallery owner smiled. "I'll insert a card in the packaging?"

"That would be nice. Say – 'With love and affection – Bernard and Theo.'"

"Perfect."

Theo and Bernard walked the short remaining distance to the restaurant, a large deck jutting out over the beach, with unobstructed views of the harbor and town pier. They were seated on the edge of the deck, just near the water, high tide lapping at the pilings underneath. The early evening golden light bounced off the buildings and boats. Theo's face was aglow.

A server came and took their drink orders and enumerated several specials. Theo leaned his arms on the table and fidgeted nervously with his napkin.

"Theo, you look restless. What's up?"

Theo doubled his napkin, rearranged the silverware, and looked evasively out over the harbor. "I have something to ask you."

"Yes?"

"I've been thinking. Wouldn't it be good for Oliver to spend some time in the States?"

"But he's so young. He doesn't travel well, you know that."

"I'm not talking about a vacation."

"You're not?"

"No. I've been thinking. Maybe we should get a place here."

"And leave Switzerland?"

"No. Jules would hunt us down. No, a second home – or perhaps a third since we have Bern and Grindelwald."

Bernard was speechless, leaning back in his chair, stroking his chin in thought.

"You're not saying anything."

"I'm just trying to process it. I never thought about it, but it makes some sense."

"Oliver could spend time here, learn the language, and develop an affinity for the States."

"But would Jules go along with it?"

"We tentatively discussed it. At first, she wasn't happy about the idea, but I explained that since she worked for Generix, she could spend time in Boston for work, too. We could travel back and forth between Bern and Boston. Zoe would love the adventure. It would be an education for her."

"What about schools and things like that?"

"We can work that all out. Maybe we spend a semester in Boston and a semester in Bern. I just want to know what you think about the idea in general."

"It's amazing. I'm a little apprehensive – it would require a lot of logistics – but I guess it could work."

"I spoke to Hans, and he doesn't think there would be a problem either."

Bernard raised his eyebrow.

"Is that a yes?"

"Tentative."

Theo smiled contently, reaching his hand over to Bernard's.

"But what about your work? How does a Swiss politician take up residence in Boston?"

"He doesn't."

"So, I don't get it."

"Well, believe it or not, I'm eligible for a new administrative post and, after the pandemic of 2020, most of us can work remotely, at least most of the time. I can check in with the office here and there but, for the most part, just log in and do my work."

Bernard looked at him with amazement.

"And get this," Theo continued. "With the new role, I'm not under the same scrutiny as before."

"What does that mean?"

"It means we could get married."

"Whaaat?" Bernard exclaimed in disbelief.

"Yes, I could officially divorce Jules and marry you, no questions asked."

"But how does that impact my work with Hans?" Bernard asked subtly regarding his spy work.

"Hans said it wouldn't be a problem. You can continue to use your position at Generix to cover. In fact, it will take some of the pressure off trying to conceal things."

"I don't get it."

"Well, if you and I are married, and you work for Generix and I for the government, there's no need to dance around my relationship with Jules. You can still run secret missions for Hans, and no one will suspect anything."

"Isn't there a conflict of interest – I working in the same agency as you?"

"My new position would be totally outside of the area Hans is in. He already cleared it."

"You've been giving this some thought and scrutiny. But I am still concerned about Jules. What is she going to think about officially divorcing? That's a big step."

"She's always wished we could regularize things better, providing more protections for Oliver. She'll be on board."

Theo pulled out a little black box from his pocket. Bernard gulped, and people at adjoining tables stopped talking, looking over at them.

"Bernard Williams, will you marry me?"

Bernard beamed a warm smile. "Oh my God, yes!" He bounced up and down in his seat.

People at adjoining tables clapped. Theo leaned over and placed the ring on Bernard's finger, giving him a kiss.

A server came over to the table with champagne and popped the cork, filling their glasses. He winked knowingly at Theo; a sign the whole proposal had been prearranged with the staff. They toasted, Bernard reaching over to Theo's hand, holding it tightly.

"I just can't believe it!" Bernard reiterated, looking intensely into Theo's watering eyes.

"We've come a long way from the first day I met you – when Zoe fell. She brought us together."

"Fate – destiny - brought us together." Bernard emphasized.

"You and your mystical stuff," Theo said in jest.

"You have to admit that just the right constellation of circumstances had to come together to make this happen." Bernard continued to press.

"Well, however it happened, I'm the luckiest man in the world."

On the edge of the Atlantic Ocean, looking across the table at his handsome Swiss fiancé, Bernard realized he had crossed many borders, learned many languages, and adjusted to different cultures around the world – but the border he had crossed to Theo just a few years ago, a perilous journey beyond his own comfort zone, ended up being a journey home, a path that opened his heart and filled his soul.

The End

Author Information

Michael Hartwig is a Boston and Provincetown based author specializing in LGBTQ stories set in historic settings around the world. The narratives are remarkable for fast-paced plots, passionate love stories, exploration of sexual identity, and evocative settings. Hartwig's books draw on his having lived in Europe, his professional work in international travel, and his college-level courses in sexual ethics and religion. Plots push boundaries around gender and family and introduce new paradigms of spirituality and magic. His novels are sensual – celebrating sexual desire, food, art, and geography.

For More Information About Author and Other Works Visit:
www.michaelhartwigauthor.com

www.ingramcontent.com/pod-product-compliance
Lightning Source LLC
Chambersburg PA
CBHW061925130726
47909CB00012B/1043